Jack Hazard: Every Villain Needs a Hero

Screenplay by:

Winston Steel

Copyright© 2020 All Rights Reserved by:

Jack Hazard Productions, Inc.

Jack Hazard® is a registered trademark of: Winston Steel L.L.L.P.

ISBN: 978-0-578-65230-6

Cover design by: Ronald Lainez

instagram.com/ronzadodesign

John Singh
President of Creative Development
Jack Hazard Productions Inc.
21346 Saint Andrews Boulevard Su. 194
Boca Raton, Florida 33433
561-446-2641

This is a work of fiction. Names, characters, businesses, places, events, locales, and incidents are either the products of the author's imagination or used in a fictitious manner. Any resemblance to actual persons, living or dead, or actual events is purely coincidental.

1

                              FADE IN:

INT. DOCTOR GORDON'S OFFICE - DAY

DOCTOR JEFFERY GORDON is in his late
fifties, wearing a spotless white lab
coat, tall, and has perfectly parted
hair.

His Medical School Diploma, and numerous
memberships to professional medical
societies grace the wall.

BILL KING is sitting across from Doctor
Gordon in his office. Bill is in his late
fifties, tall, of medium build, and
slightly balding up front.

He wipes the perspiration off his neatly
trimmed mustache. He is wearing a freshly
starched, blue, long-sleeved dress shirt.

Bill's black pants are pleated, with a
black leather belt and chrome buckle. His
monk strap shoes gleam.

                    BILL
Look Doctor Gordon, I understand my
Granddaughter Kimberly is on a
waiting list to receive a kidney.

                    DOCTOR GORDON
You have to understand it is illegal to
pay someone for a kidney.

                    BILL
With her juvenile diabetes, she simply
can't wait that long. Can we go overseas
to purchase a kidney?

                    DOCTOR GORDON
You have to understand this is going to
cost a lot of money.

                    BILL
How much?

                    DOCTOR GORDON
Sixty thousand dollars.

                    BILL
Doctor Gordon, if you find a kidney for
my Granddaughter, I will gladly pay you
sixty thousand dollars.

                    DOCTOR GORDON
I have some connections across the border
in Mexico. I will have to take it in
full.

Lieutenant Bill King writes out a CHECK.

                    DILL
That's fine.

                    DOCTOR GORDON
Lieutenant, I will call Christine, when
your Grand Daughter's kidney is ready for
transplant.

3

                    BILL
Thank you, Doctor Gordon, I appreciate
this. Please don't mention this to
anyone.

                    DOCTOR GORDON
Lieutenant that makes two of us.

                    BILL
Thanks Doc, have a good day.

                    DOCTOR GORDON
Same to you.

Bill closes the door to Doctor Gordon's
office; DOCTOR GORDON picks up the PHONE
and dials.

                    DOCTOR GORDON
Ranjeet, I'm going to need a kidney for a
female, Type O negative.

EXT. PARKING LOT OF RETAIL STORE - DAY

Bill walks across the street where his
PICK-UP is parked, and gets in.

INT. BILL KING'S PICK-UP - DAY

While adjusting his rear-view mirror Bill
notices TWO ARMED MASKED MEN at the
entrance of a bank, and dials NINE-ONE-
ONE on his CELL PHONE.

INT. 911 OPERATOR'S DESK - DAY

The 911 OPERATOR is in SHERIFF'S UNIFORM
receives Bill King's emergency call. With
other OPERATORS and CONTROL CENTER in
background.

INTERCUT AS NEEDED - BILL AND 911
OPERATOR ON PHONE

                    911 OPERATOR
NINE-ONE-ONE, what is your emergency?

                    BILL
This is Lieutenant King with Seventh
Precinct. We have a robbery in progress
on First Avenue and Main Street at
National Bank.

Two masked males are wearing body armor
dressed in black. Each has a slung
shotgun, and assault rifle at the ready.

                    911 OPERATOR
Lieutenant King, Special Weapons and
Tactics have been alerted, as well as
Aviation.

Maintain a defensive posture until
the Tactical Area Commander arrives.

                    BILL
Thanks.

Lieutenant Bill King hangs up on the 911

Operator. He dials his cell phone.

INT. JACK HAZARD'S PATROL CAR - DAY

JACK HAZARD is in his early twenties, of average height, muscular build, blue eyes, and sports chestnut brown hair. He is a sergeant with Precinct Seven.

Jack is in his patrol uniform and driving up front, with two FEMALE POLICE OFFICERS sitting in the rear. Jack receives a call on his CELL PHONE.

INTERCUT AS NEEDED - BILL AND JACK ON CELL PHONE

                    BILL
Jack, where are you?

                    JACK
I'm on patrol with two rookies in the back. Why?

Over Jack's Patrol Car's radio, the EMERGENCY DISPATCHER broadcasts the emergency announcement to all patrol cars.

          EMERGENCY DISPATCHER (V.O.)
Robbery in progress on First Avenue and Main Street at National Bank. Two masked males are wearing body armor and dressed in black.

Each has a slung shotgun, and assault rifle at the ready. Special Weapons and Tactics, and Aviation has been mobilized.

Switch from patrol channels to emergency channel eight. Be alert to all emergency broadcasts, dawn all tactical gear immediately.

                    JACK
Bill I'm on my way.

Jack hangs up his cell phone.

INT. JACK HAZARD'S PATROL CAR - DAY

Jack places his cell phone on top of the dash board and turns on his SIRENS and LIGHT BAR and speeds off.

INT. BILL KING'S PICK-UP - DAY

Bill places his cell phone back in his pocket.

EXT. HELICOPTER PAD - DAY

A Police Aviation Pilot pulls down his HELMET VISOR and pulls on the YOLK of a POLICE HELICOPTER and lifts off.

INT. BANK - DAY

BANK ROBBER #1 and BANK ROBBER #2 enter the bank.

BANK ROBBER #1

Don't trigger any silent alarms! Shut the fuck up! Lay face down on the floor!

BANK ROBBER #2 shoots a SECURITY GUARD in the torso with his SHOT GUN.

He then runs up to the fallen security guard; and shoots him again at point-blank range, to the head.

He vaults over the bank teller's counter and grabs the BANK MANAGER who is wearing a THREE-PIECE SUIT and grabs him by the collar.

BANK ROBBER #2

You know what to give me and hurry it up!

The bank manager opens up the BANK VAULT and begins putting money in the DUFFEL BAG. Bank Robber #2 rips the bag out of the manager's hands and zips it up.

He slings it over his shoulder, and vaults back over the teller's counter.

Bank Robber #1 grabs a PREGNANT WOMAN by the neck laying on her side, she is forced to stand up at gunpoint.

PREGNANT WOMAN

I have a baby! I have a baby!

BANK ROBBER #1
Shut up! Nobody cares lady!

EXT. PARKING LOT RETAIL STORE ACROSS FROM
BANK - DAY

Bill runs up with his BADGE out, and
waves down the PATROL CARS as they enter
the parking lot.

BILL
Align your cars across bumper to bumper.
We got a robbery in progress, across the
street!

EXT. PATROL CAR DRIVER'S SIDE DOOR - DAY

Bill then runs back to the last Patrol
Car.

BILL
Take your car and block off the
parking lot entrance. Run into the store
and tell the store manager the bank is
being robbed.

Tell the customers to use the rear exit,
and pick up their cars tomorrow.

POLICE PATROL CAR DRIVER
Got it.

The PATROL CAR DRIVER speeds off.

EXT. BANK - DAY

The robbers with their hostage exit the
bank. They spot the police, and begin
firing their weapons at the patrol cars.

EXT. PARKING LOT RETAIL STORE ACROSS FROM
BANK - DAY

POLICE are positioned behind their
vehicles across the street with their
GUNS drawn.

Numerous tires burst, wind shields are
shattered, trunk locks are shot out
causing trunks to open.

One OFFICER ducks down just as a patrol
car window breaks causing bits of glass
to fall down his collar, and on his hair.

                    BILL
Get down! Hold your fire they have
a hostage!

EXT. STREET IN FRONT OF BANK/ACROSS
RETAIL STORE - DAY

Robber #2 fires his ASSAULT RIFLE at the
Police. While Robber #1 drags the
pregnant woman by the neck, at gunpoint.

The policemen hold their fire and duck
behind their cars.

                    ROBBER #1
Car jack that bastard and cover me!

Robber #2 shoots in the air over a pickup
truck. The DRIVER of the car BRAKES.
Robber #2 then runs over and opens the
driver's side door.

                    ROBBER #2
Get out!

Robber #2 unbuckles the driver's seat
belt and throws the DRIVER out of the
car. The Driver falls down then runs a
way.

Robber #2 gets in the driver's seat; and
drives the car at a slow pace, parallel
to Robber #1, providing cover from
incoming police fire.

Robber #1 starts spraying the Patrol Cars
with bullets; as he drags the pregnant
hostage by the neck. He then releases the
hostage.

                    ROBBER #1
Get away from me!

The pregnant woman falls to her knees and
hobbles off. Robber #1 walking astride
the pickup truck's bed continues firing
at the police.

INT. CAPTAIN JACKSON'S PATROL CAR - DAY

CAPTAIN RICHARD JACKSON is driving to the scene in his PATROL CAR while listening to the POLICE RADIO.

Driving up to an intersection he is startled that he is across from the hijacked pickup truck and BANK ROBBER #1.

Captain Jackson slams on the BRAKES; his wind shield is shattered from incoming fire. Captain Jackson is slumped over the steering wheel.

The car comes to a dead stop when it turns into the sidewalk curb.

I/E. JACK'S PATROL CAR - DAY

Police Academy Graduate DEBORAH CASSANOVA is in her late teens. Blonde, blue eyes, and beautiful, she nervously clutches the handle of her handgun.

The other female officer, stares at Deborah's handgun. She takes a deep breath and then places her hand on her own handgun.

                    JACK
Ladies, I need you to get out of the car and cover me! I'm going to drive over to Rich!

                    DEBORAH
Sergeant, what do we do?

                     JACK
What do you mean, what do we do? You do
what they taught you at the Police
Academy! Lie flat on the ground and lay
suppressive fire!

Deborah Casanova and the other female
officer exit Jack's Patrol Car, with both
rear doors open.

They lie down on the sidewalk, and begin
firing at the robbers. Jack drives off to
rescue Rich; with the rear passenger
doors swinging open and shut.

                     JACK
God, I hate rookies they're so stupid!

Jack's car screeches to a halt; and slams
his car in park, perpendicular to the
rear of Jackson's Patrol Car. He exits
leaving his door open.

EXT. CAPTAIN RICHARD JACKSON'S PATROL
CAR - DAY

Jack runs and slips on motor oil, face
front. He belly crawls to Captain
Jackson's Patrol Car.

He repeatedly attempts to open the door
handle, but it is locked. Jack crouches

and unlocks the door through the broken
driver's side window.

He opens the door, and unfastens Captain
Jackson's seat belt.

Jack throws Captain Jackson over his
shoulder causing BLOOD to drip, and TEETH
to fall to the pavement, from Captain
Jackson. Jack runs back to his patrol
car.

INT. JACK'S PATROL CAR - DAY

Jack carries Captain Jackson through the
front cabin and shoves him in the front
passenger seat.

He slams the driver door shut; and races
back to the retail store parking lot,
with both rear doors swinging ajar.

Jack grabs his patrol's car radio
receiver.

                    JACK
               (into radio)
I got the Captain! I got the Captain!

He drops the receiver on the floor and
his cell phone falls off the dash board.

EXT. PARKING LOT RETAIL STORE ACROSS FROM
BANK - DAY

Bill runs towards Jack's patrol car and helps carry Captain Jackson out of the passenger seat.

MEDIC #1 and MEDIC #2 run over with a WHEELED STRETCHER and place Captain Jackson on top of it. Jack, Bill and the Medics rush the Captain to the ambulance.

EXT. AMBULANCE - DAY

Medic #2 opens the rear doors of the Ambulance.

                    BILL
Is he alive?

Jack remains silent. They all duck down simultaneously, when a bullet ricochets off the ambulance and breaks a tail light.

EXT. PARKING LOT RETAIL STORE - DAY

A SWAT ARMORED PERSONNEL CARRIER rolls off the bed of a SEMI-TRUCK next to the Ambulance and exits the parking lot in pursuit of the Robbers.

EXT. SWAT ARMORED PERSONNEL CARRIER - DAY

A SWAT member in the turret of an ARMORED PERSONNEL CARRIER stares through the scope of his heavy machine gun at the pickup truck being driven by Robber #2.

He squeezes a continuous line of fire at the truck's hood causing it to blow off.

Then decapitates the head of Robber #2 causing blood to splatter throughout the cabin.

He then draws a line of fire to the rear of the pick-up bed; causing a second explosion that breaks windows of nearby buildings.

Robber #1 is thrown by the shock wave on his back.

Robber #1 rolls over places a shotgun underneath his chin, and pulls the trigger.

EXT. CAPTAIN RICH JACKSON'S FUNERAL - DAY

Captain Jackson's closed coffin lies to the right of the podium on the dais. All the officers from the precinct are wearing their FORMAL DRESS BLUE UNIFORMS.

A sea of MOURNERS are dressed in black. THE MAYOR, and his DEPUTY MAYOR are standing up with their hands over their hearts.

CHIEF MCCORMICK is in his late seventies, and LIEUTENANT CHIEF ANDREWS is in his early sixties; both are standing at attention and saluting.

The CAPTAIN OF THE FIRING PARTY shouts
the cadence of a three-volley salute to
the SEVEN MAN RIFLE DETAIL. Afterwards
the BUGLER begins to play taps.

                    CAPTAIN OF THE FIRING PARTY
Ready, aim, fire!

GUN SHOT

Ready, aim, fire!

GUN SHOT

Ready, aim, fire!

GUN SHOT

Present Arms.

TAPS PLAY

EXT. COFFEE SHOP - DAY

Sergeant Jack Hazard opens the door for
Chief McCormick, Lieutenant Chief
Andrews, and Lieutenant Bill King.

INT. COFFEE SHOP - DAY

They are greeted by a HOSTESS and led to
their booth by a WAITER.

Chief McCormick gestures with his hand to
Lieutenant Bill King and Sergeant Jack

Hazard to slide into the booth opposite him, and Lieutenant Chief Andrews.

                    WAITER
The usual gentlemen?

They all nod. Lieutenant Chief Andrews hands PROMOTION LETTERS to both Jack and Bill.

                 CHIEF MCCORMICK
Since Captain Jackson's passing the Commission has promoted you Lieutenant King to Captain, and Sergeant Hazard you have been promoted to Lieutenant.

I know the loss of Captain Jackson was unexpected, but when we all signed up for this job, we realized our lives can be taken away at any moment.

The waiter brings four COFFEE MUGS and a COFFEE POT, and begins serving the men.

On Monday at four o'clock be ready in your dress blue uniforms, for your promotion ceremony.

We will be there along, with public affairs. Don't forget to bring your friends and family.

                    BILL
Chief, I appreciate it.

                    JACK
Chief, we won't let you down.

                    CHIEF MCCORMICK
It's all right. Let's hope this is
the last funeral of the year.

INT. JACK'S HOME - DAY

STACY CLINTON in her early twenties, has
jet black hair down to her waist, she is
drop dead gorgeous, and naturally
voluptuous.

Stacy is dressed in a translucent
camisole. She is snorting a line of WHITE
POWDER through a STRAW off the kitchen
table.

Jack opens the front door and walks in on
Stacy, his mouth drops.

                    JACK
Babe, what the fuck are you doing? I
thought you were going quit that shit?

                    STACY
Hun, I'm sorry, but I was so tired
from dancing last night. I just
needed a little.

                    JACK
Babe, you're not going to have to
worry about being tired. Because you're
going to be fucking dead if you don't
stop this!

                    STACY
Honey, I'm sorry, I'm going to get help.
How was the funeral? How's Bill?

Jack sits down at the table.

                    JACK
Bill is fine, Chief told us our
promotions were approved by the Police
Commission and the City Board of
Supervisors.

                    STACY
A promotion!

                    JACK
Bill got promoted to captain, Captain
Jackson's old position. I got promoted to
lieutenant, and will be taking over
Bill's position as Precinct Lieutenant.

                    STACY
Does that mean we could move, and
get married?

                    JACK
Stacy, I told you we are not getting

married until you stop putting that shit
up your nose.

Stacy sits on Jack's lap caresses his ear
and then whispers in his ear inaudibly.
Jack lifts up Stacy with her legs wrapped
around his waist.

                    JACK
Let the good times roll.

Jack enters his bedroom with Stacy, and
then slams the door shut.

INT. PRECINCT ORDERLY ROOM - DAY

Lieutenant Bill King has just been
promoted to captain, and Sergeant Jack
Hazard has been promoted to lieutenant.

Cameras flash across the faces of Bill,
and Jack in the precinct orderly room.
All the officers are in a celebratory
mood in their FORMAL DRESS BLUE UNIFORMS.

                    CHIEF MCCORMICK
Precinct dismissed.

Bill's Granddaughter KIMBERLY CARTER who
is age four, has her blonde hair braided
in a ponytail. She jumps into Bill's
arms.

                    KIMBERLY
I love you Grandpa!

Kimberly hugs Bill and gives him a kiss
on his cheek.

                    BILL
I love you Kimberly.

Bill then gently puts her down, and gives
Kimberly a kiss on the forehead. Bill's
wife SARAH KING is in her early fifties;
has shoulder length blonde hair, without
a sign of gray.

Sarah walks up in a gray women's two
button blazer. Sarah gives Bill a kiss on
the lips and long embrace.

Bill's daughter is in her early twenties,
CHRISTINE CARTER is wearing a red dress.
She is bedecked in platinum jewelry.

Tall and blonde, she has her hair in a
braided bun. She kisses her father, Bill
kisses Christine on her cheek and hugs
her.

                  CHRISTINE
Dad, Congratulations.

Extremely tall and muscular; son-in-law
DAVE CARTER walks up to Bill in a blue
pin striped three-piece suit.

Dave's University of Southern California;
Two-Thousand and Four, Football National

Champion Ring, scintillates as he shakes
hands with Bill, and gives him a hug.
Despite being in his early forties, he
looks much younger.

                    DAVE
Bill, it's great that you have been
promoted to captain.

                    BILL
Dave thank you. I'm glad you could
make it.

Chief McCormick walks up to Bill to shake
his hand.

                    BILL
Chief, thank you again.

                CHIEF MCCORMICK
Bill it's no trouble. I know you and Jack
are going to do a great job. I wish I
could stay for refreshments, but I have
to attend a city budgetary hearing for
the department.

Chief McCormick keeps talking to newly
promoted Captain Bill King while Jack
stands by and watches. HANNAH the
precinct secretary, walks into the
orderly room.

                    HANNAH
Jack you have a phone call. Tookie
is on the line.

                    JACK
Tookie?

                   HANNAH
Yes, Lieutenant she is call parked on
line sixty-six.

Jack walks out of the orderly room.

INT. JACK'S OFFICE - DAY

Jack walks up to his desk, picks-up the
phone, and dials.

                    JACK
Good day, Lieutenant Jack Hazard
speaking.

                TOOKIE (V.O.)
                (over phone)
Jack is that you? It's Tookie.

                    JACK
Tookie didn't I tell you not to
call me here, unless it's important.

                TOOKIE (V.O.)
                (over phone)
Jack something is wrong. Me and Stacy
were supposed to leave for a movie at
five o'clock today.

I've been knocking on the door for

fifteen minutes, and Stacy won't come to
the door.

I tried calling her on her cell phone six
times, but she won't answer. This is not
like her.

                    JACK
Tookie listen I'm going to give Stacy a
call. If I don't get in touch with her,
I'll be there in forty minutes.

Jack hangs up on Tookie then dials Stacy.
A HARD ROCK ring tone plays before the
out-going message.

A different HARD ROCK tune plays in the
background of Stacy's outgoing message.

                 STACY (V.O.)
               (outgoing message)
"Hi, you've reached Stacy Clinton,
please leave a message, and I'll
try to get back to you."

                    JACK
                 (into phone)
Hey Stacy, it's Jack. Call me a soon as
you can, and give Tookie a call.

You were supposed to go with her to the
movies at five o'clock; and remember
babe, call me.

Jack hangs up the phone and walks

back to the orderly room.

INT. PRECINCT ORDERLY ROOM - DAY

Bill is still chatting with his family when Jack approaches him.

                    JACK
Say Bill, Stacy isn't feeling well. I'm going to go home to see her.

                    SARAH
Is she all right?

                    JACK
I'm sure she's fine. She's just a bit under the weather.

                    BILL
No problem, the ceremony is already over. I'll see you tomorrow.

                    JACK
All right, well Mrs. King, Dave, Christine, take care.

                    KIMBERLY
Bye, Jack.

                    JACK
Take care Kimberly, I love you. Jack blows a kiss and waves at Kimberly. Kimberly blows a kiss back. Jack then exits the orderly room.

EXT. JACK'S HOUSE DRIVEWAY - DAY

Jack pulls up to his house. Upon arriving he sees Tookie smoking a CIGARETTE; sitting in front of his door.

Tookie's yellow crochet halter top, peeks through his blue leather jacket which compliments his blue platform pumps.

His knees are straddled up through his red mini skirt.

                    TOOKIE
It's about time you got here. I've been waiting for nearly an hour.

                    JACK
Sorry Tookie, I was busy at work. That's why I'm late meeting, my favorite, friendly, neighborhood, pre-operative transvestite.

Now can you get up so I can open the door.

                    TOOKIE
There is no need to act snippy, with me.

                    JACK
Get up, I need to open up.

Jack punches in the combination to the front door lock.

INT. JACK'S HOME - DAY

Tookie and Jack enter. All is quiet except for the ceiling fan. Tookie pulls up a chair. Jack walks to his bedroom

                    TOOKIE
God damn, it's freezing in here.

INT. - JACK'S BEDROOM - DAY

Jack walks in where he notices Stacy lying face down on his bed wearing a thong, and is topless.

On her lower back, she has a pair of horizontal six-inch incisions, on opposing sides.

Blood is all over the white bed sheet, and smeared on her body. Jack shouts at Tookie, who then rushes into the bedroom.

                    JACK
What the hell! Tookie call 911!

Tookie enters the bedroom.

                    TOOKIE
What happened!

                    JACK
Tookie call 911!

Tookie runs out of the room. Jack turns

Stacy face front, feels for a pulse on her carotid artery. Jack begins CPR. Starting compressions, he turns his head to shout at Tookie in the kitchen.

                    JACK
Tookie open up the door, so the medics know where to go!

                    TOOKIE (O.S.)
I can't hear you! I am on the phone with 911!
                    JACK
               (louder)
I said open up the front door so the medics can come in!

                    TOOKIE (O.S.)
Okay!

INT. - JACK'S KITCHEN - DAY

Tookie is clutching the phone with both hands.

911 OPERATOR'S DESK - DAY

The 911 OPERATOR in SHERIFF'S UNIFORM is on her headset with Tookie.

INTERCUT AS NEEDED - TOOKIE AND 911 OPERATOR ON PHONE

                    TOOKIE
               (into phone)

Are you still there? Should I open up the
door, so the medics can come in the
apartment?

INT. 911 OPERATOR'S DESK - DAY

                    911 OPERATOR
               (into phone)
Yes, but make sure you get right back on
the phone with me, until the medics
arrive.

INT. JACK'S KITCHEN - DAY

Tookie drops the phone receiver on the
counter and runs to the front door.

INT. 911 OPERATOR'S DESK - DAY

The 911 Operator is startled and grimaces
when she hears the phone receiver drop on
the kitchen counter top.

INT. JACK'S HOME - DAY

Tookie opens the door. She then runs back
to the kitchen and picks up the phone
receiver.

INT. JACK'S KITCHEN - DAY

                    TOOKIE
               (into phone)
Okay. I'm back.

INT. JACK'S BEDROOM - DAY

Jack continues with chest compressions,
causing Stacy's lacerations to bleed all
over the bed sheets. Ambulance SIRENS are
blaring in the background.

Jack pinches her nose and lift Stacy's
chin to perform mouth to mouth.

Two MEDICS enter the bedroom, with their
MEDIC BAGS on top of a COLLAPSIBLE
WHEELED STRETCHER.

They find Jack with blood all over his
police dress blue uniform.

                    MEDIC #3
Sir, what happened? Are you a police
officer?

                    JACK
Yes, I'm Lieutenant Hazard. I found my
girlfriend with two cuts on her back,
face down.

She doesn't have a pulse. I tried
CPR, but she isn't responding.

MEDIC #3 places a NECK BRACE around
Stacy, MEDIC #4 pushes the stretcher
beside the bed. Both medics lift Stacy's
body onto the stretcher.

                    MEDIC #3
Get ready to lift on the count of
three. ONE. TWO. THREE. Lift.

MEDIC #4 then places a BAG-VALVE-MASK
VENTILATOR over Stacy's mouth and begins
squeezing the bag repeatedly.

                    MEDIC #3
If you like Lieutenant, you can follow us
to University Hospital.

                    JACK
I'll be right behind you.

The medics then wheel Stacy out of the
bedroom. Jack walks out to the living
room where he finds Tookie crying on the
sofa.

INT. JACK'S HOUSE LIVING ROOM - DAY

                    TOOKIE
Is she going to make it?

                    JACK
Of course, she's going to make it!
Now, stop crying, and let's go. We have
to go to University Hospital.

EXT. HOSPITAL - DAY

The AMBULANCE arrives outside the
Emergency Room entrance.

Medic #3 exits the driver side and slams the door shut. Medic #3 runs to the rear of the ambulance and opens the barn doors.

Medic #4 is compressing the BAG-VALVE-MASK VENTILATOR; the Medics lift Stacy's stretcher out of the ambulance and roll her through the entrance doors.

EXT. HOSPITAL PARKING LOT - DAY

Jack and Tookie pull up to the hospital parking lot. Getting out of JACK'S CAR, Tookie falls out of the passenger seat.

Jack rushes to the other side of the car to pick Tookie up.

                    JACK
Tookie your too big to walk in those stripper pumps. Get up! I don't need two people visiting the emergency room today!

Tookie grabs Jack's hand and stands up. Jack and Tookie then run over to the Emergency Room lobby entrance.

INT. EMERGENCY ROOM LOBBY - DAY

Jack and Tookie enter the Emergency Room lobby.

INT. EMERGENCY ROOM ADMISSIONS DESK - DAY

They approach NURSE NORRIS at the
admission's desk.

                    NURSE NORRIS
Are you all right? Are you in need of any
assistance?

                    TOOKIE
Yes and no.

Jack pushes Tookie aside.

                    JACK
Yes, Nurse Norris my fiance Stacy
Clinton, was just admitted to ER with
lacerations on her back.

                    NURSE NORRIS
Let me first scan your IDs so I can make
you a visitor's band. I'll then try to
find out what's her status.

Jack and Tookie hand their IDENTIFICATION
CARDS to Nurse Norris. Nurse Norris walks
to the back office. Tookie grabs Jack's
arm and whispers into his ear.

                    TOOKIE
You proposed to Stacy, and she didn't
even tell me. Did you buy her a ring?

Jack whispers in Tookie's ear.

                    JACK
Hell no. Both of you are still shoving
sugar up your nose. The only reason why I
told the nurse that, is so we can see
Stacy.

Nurse Norris then walks back again to the
admission's desk, with Tookie's ID in
hand.

INSERT - TOOKIE'S WORKER ID

"Heading: NAUGHTY NUDE CABARET
 Name: John Rizzo
 Position: General Manager
 Address: Director's choice"

BACK TO NURSE NORRIS

                  NURSE NORRIS

I'm sorry Mr. Rizzo; but do you have a
Government ID I can scan, so I can issue
you your visitor's band?

Tookie rummages through his LARGE PINK
PURSE.

He hands Nurse Norris his DRIVERS
LICENSE; with a WRAPPED PROPHYLACTIC
stuck on the back and WHITE PARTICLES on
the front of the license.

Nurse Norris blows off the white
particles.

                    NURSE NORRIS
I'm sorry Mr. Rizzo. I do not need this.

Nurse Norris hands back Tookie the
wrapped prophylactic.

                    TOOKIE
I'm sorry. You can call me Tookie.

                    NURSE NORRIS
Sure...Tookie, Lieutenant Hazard, I
will be right back with the bands.

Nurse Norris comes back, with both of
their BANDS. Nurse Norris places them on
Tookie's and Jack's wrist and then hands
back their identification cards.

                    NURSE NORRIS
Lieutenant Hazard, if you and Tookie can
take a seat. The lead surgical nurse and
attending doctor; will come and see you,
after they are done with Stacy.

                    TOOKIE
How long will it take before Stacy
is released? Will she be able to
come home today?

                    NURSE NORRIS
Mam, I'm mean Sir, I... I... I mean
Tookie. I'm not going to lie to you.

It could take six hours, it could take
sixteen hours. It all depends how serious
are the injuries.

                    JACK
Tookie, we have to sit down and wait.

INT. EMERGENCY ROOM LOBBY - DAY

Jack and Tookie walk to their seats in
the emergency room lobby. Hours pass;
Jack and Tookie talk, read magazines, and
watch TV to pass the time.

INT. EMERGENCY ROOM LOBBY - NIGHT

Tookie has fallen asleep on Jack's
shoulder. Jack has his head leaned back
against the wall snoring. Nurse Norris
wakes up Jack, and Tookie.

                    NURSE NORRIS
I'm sorry Lieutenant Hazard, has the
attending surgeon spoke to you already?

                    JACK
No.

                    NURSE NORRIS
Let me talk to Nurse Wellington.

The Head Surgical Nurse, NURSE WELLINGTON
walks up to Lieutenant Hazard, in
OPERATING ROOM SCRUBS.

                    NURSE WELLINGTON
Lieutenant Hazard, I am terrible
sorry about the delay. If you follow me,
Doctor Bachman will see you now.

                    JACK
No problem.

                    TOOKIE
Thank God. It's been so long.

Nurse Wellington, leads Jack and Tookie
to a conference room where DOCTOR BACHMAN
is sitting. Doctor Bachman stands up, and
invites everyone to take a seat.

INT. HOSPITAL CONFERENCE ROOM

                    DOCTOR BACHMAN
Lieutenant, Tookie, please take a seat.
Lieutenant Hazard I am sorry, but there
was nothing I could do for Stacy.

                    TOOKIE
What do you mean?

Jack's eyes dilate, and a bead of sweat
rolls down his cheek.

                    DOCTOR BACHMAN
Upon admittance she was already dead.
Her core body temperature was 82.2
degrees Fahrenheit; far below 98.4
degrees, normal body temperature.

However; we did find out through
Radiology that the two lacerations on her
back, were in fact incisions.

Someone removed her kidneys. This is what
caused her to bleed to death.

Jack slowly stands up in shock, and then
vomits on Doctor Bachman's face, and
glasses.

Doctor Bachman stands up and catches him,
just as he passes out. Tookie puts his
hands to his face and cries hysterically.

                    TOOKIE
No! No! No!

                    NURSE WELLINGTON
Doctor, I will call for a stretcher.

                    DOCTOR BACHMAN
Please hurry!

INT. JACK'S HOSPITAL ROOM - DAY

SUPER IN/OUT: "THE NEXT DAY"

Bill is sitting in a chair next to Jack's
hospital bed. Jack wakes up, trying to
make out the blur that is Bill.

                    JACK
Bill?

                    BILL
Who else do you think it is? Do I
look like a pre-op transvestite
named Tookie?

                    JACK
No. You are far prettier than that
cross dresser.

                    BILL
Jack, you went into diabetic shock.

                    JACK
I have diabetes?

                    BILL
Yeah, if you went into diabetic shock it
means you have diabetes.

                    JACK
So, that makes two of us me and Kimberly.

                    BILL
Unfortunately, yes.

                    JACK
How did you find this out?

                    BILL
I read your bed chart.

Bill holds up JACK'S BED CHART at the
foot of Jack's Hospital Bed.

                    BILL
I don't know if you remember, but both of
Stacy's kidneys were removed. As a
result, Doctor Bachman referred this case
to the City Coroner for an autopsy.

I already contacted James Woolsworthy;
Chief Prosecutor for the District to open
up an investigation. This isn't the first
time this has happened.

                    JACK
Happened?

                    BILL
It seems to be a trend. The coroner had
two other bodies brought in just this
week, cut up the same way. Their kidneys,
gone.

                    JACK
Jesus Christ, I didn't know kidneys were
such a hot product. Where were the bodies
found?

                    BILL
Both of the bodies were found in an alley
adjacent to, Lexington Avenue and One-
Hundred and Twenty-Fifth Street.

Although, there is no connection between
the two vagrants and Stacy, three people
with their kidneys removed is no
coincidence.

George, Ninth Precinct's Captain tried to call you last night. Crime Scene Investigation had to collect evidence at your house.

Needless to say, you couldn't answer your cell phone, because you were too busy barfing all over Doctor Bachman.

                    JACK
Did they find anything of use?

                    BILL
They did the usual. They compared fingerprints of you, Stacy, and Tookie.

Your bed, carpet, and other items with Stacy's blood on it were taken into evidence. Other than that, your apartment is in great shape.

                    JACK
I never heard of this happening before.

                    BILL
I haven't seen anything like it either.

                    JACK
Speaking of kidneys, how is the search going for Kimberly? Have they found a match for her kidney transplant?

                    BILL
No, not yet.

                    JACK
So, who is covering me at Precinct Seven?

                    BILL
Sergeant Sullivan is going to be in
charge of the precinct while you are on
sick leave.

Bill stands up from his chair.

                    JACK
Sullivan is a good guy, we both graduated
from the police academy together.

Bill kisses Jack on the forehead then
walks over and opens the door.

                    BILL
Take care kid. Oh, and by the way, Tookie
is down in the lobby waiting for you.

                    JACK
Tookie?

                    BILL
Who else?

Bill then exits.

INT. HOSPITAL LOBBY ELEVATOR
LANDING/DISCHARGE DESK - DAY

Jack walks out of the lobby floor
elevator, and goes over to the hospital
discharge desk.

                    JACK
Hi, I'm Jack Hazard I need to check out.

                NURSE RODRIGUEZ
Sure, please read your release before
signing below on the tablet.

He signs the COMPUTER TABLET with a
STYLUS, and hands it back to NURSE
RODRIGUEZ. He then walks to the lobby and
spots Tookie reading a FASHION MAGAZINE.

INT. HOSPITAL LOBBY - DAY

                   TOOKIE
Are you better now?

                    JACK
I sure hope so. This week hasn't
been a joy ride.

                   TOOKIE
Jack, I need to talk to you about Stacy,
its important. Can we go somewhere to
eat?

                    JACK
Is the taco joint at the corner of the
street okay?

                    TOOKIE
That's fine.

Jack and Tookie exit the hospital lobby
doors.

I/E FAST FOOD RESTAURANT - DAY

Jack and Tookie pull up to the taco fast
food restaurant. Jack and Tookie enter,
people immediately begin to stare at
Tookie.

Tookie sits down, Jack returns with FOOD
and sits at the table across from Tookie.
They eat.

                    JACK
What did you want to tell me about Stacy?

                    TOOKIE
There were these strange men who
approached me and Stacy at the strip
club. They looked weird.

                    JACK
What was wrong with them?

                    TOOKIE
Well, they had long unshaven beards, and
shiny bangles.

                    JACK
Where they Hasidic Jews? Did they have a

big, black, broad brim, hat?

                    TOOKIE
No. No. They had towels wrapped around
their heads.

                    JACK
Towels?

                    TOOKIE
Yeah...towels, you know like the weirdos
who always work at the gas stations, and
convenient stores.

Jack breaks out laughing, spitting out
soda.

                    JACK
Tookie, those people are Sikhs.

                    TOOKIE
No; they weren't sick, they looked
healthy.

                    JACK
No, Tookie those people are called
Sikhs. They practice a religion called
Sikhism.

They wear turbans and wear a bangle on
their wrist, it's part of their religion.
Kind of like how I wear a Cross.

Jack pulls out his GOLD CRUCIFIX ON A
BHAT CHAIN then places

it back in his shirt.

                    TOOKIE
Well any way these guys, walked in to the
strip club, and approached Stacy for a
lap dance. They had a lot of money.

So, Stacy took them back to the VIP room.
While she was giving them a lap dance,
she started bleeding.

                    JACK
Was is that time of the month?

                    TOOKIE
No stupid, she had a nose bleed.

                    JACK
Gee... I wonder what would cause that?

                    TOOKIE
Any way, they told Stacy not to worry.
They're medical students.

One of them, grabbed two cocktail napkins
and told Stacy to pinch her nose, with a
napkin, sit down, and lean forward.

                    JACK
Big deal. They know first aid.

                    TOOKIE
Jack, it is not that common for a guy at
a strip club to actually give a shit
about a dancer.

Let alone tipping her a thousand dollars.

                    JACK
A thousand dollars?

                    TOOKIE
Of course, a thousand dollars. She has a
thick juicy ass, big natural tits, and a
face of an angel. Now what man could
resist that Jack?

                    JACK
I guess, I'm guilty as charged.

                    TOOKIE
They came back the very next day, and
that's when they gave Stacy the
proposition.

                    JACK
What proposition? Are you telling me
Stacy was selling her ass on the side for
cash?
                    TOOKIE
They told her that a girl needed a kidney
transplant to live. So, if Stacy would
donate just one of her kidneys, she would
get fifty-thousand dollars in cash.

So of course, she said yes. Don't you
know how much cocaine fifty-thousand
dollars can buy?

Jack jumps off his seat enraged, and
PISTOL whips Tookie on the side of his

head causing his wig to fly off. Tookie
breaks down crying, while people run out
of the restaurant in fear. The staff
freezes behind the counter silent.

                    JACK
You fucking idiot! You knew Stacy was
going to sell her kidney, and you didn't
even tell me!

                    TOOKIE
I'm sorry! I'm sorry! I didn't think she
was going to do it, until it was too
late!

Jack puts his PISTOL back in his holster,
sits down, slumps forward in his seat,
and cups his hands over his face.

Tookie picks up his wig off the floor,
puts it on, and straightens it out.

                    JACK
Come on Tookie let's go.

                    TOOKIE
Can you take me home?

                    JACK
Yeah.

Jack and Tookie leave the restaurant.

I/E. JACK'S CAR - NIGHT

Jack starts his car, and rolls down the
windows, Tookie lights up a cigarette.
Jack drives down the street.

                    TOOKIE
Say, can we stop at Lexington and One
Hundred and Twenty Fifth Street? I need
to pick something up.

Jack SLAMS ON THE BRAKES. Tookie's head
hits the console. Jack takes off his
seat belt runs to Tookie's passenger side
seat and throws him out of the car.

                    TOOKIE
What the fuck are you doing asshole!

                    JACK
Asshole! Asshole! You don't give a fuck
about anything; except sniffing coke up
your nose!

You don't give a fuck about yourself! You
don't give a fuck about me! You didn't
even give a fuck about Stacy!

The only thing you care about is cocaine!

                    TOOKIE
Are you stupid? You think you can just
stop and quit?

                    JACK
You better quit, or else you're going to
be a dead drag queen!

TOOKIE
I'm going to get help... I'm going to get
help.

JACK
Look, check yourself into the city's
detox center. You're the only one who can
do it. I'm not the one who's an addict,
and I can't quit for you!

Jack walks back to the car, and REVS THE
ENGINE. Tookie yells from the side walk.

TOOKIE
How am I going to get back home?

JACK
You have legs! Walk!

Tookie takes off one of his high heels,
and throws it at Jack's car as he speeds
off.

TOOKIE
Dick!

INT. JACK'S HOME - NIGHT

Jack opens up the front door of his
House; Jack walks to his bedroom and
opens the door.

INT. JACK'S BEDROOM - NIGHT

He turns on the room light and stares at

the exposed bare concrete floor where crime scene investigators have cut out the carpet, and removed his bed.

He turns on his POLISHED BRASS LAMP that is sitting on his night stand. He walks towards the bathroom.

INT. JACK'S BATHROOM - NIGHT

Jack takes his clothes off and puts them in the LAUNDRY HAMPER. He shaves his face and takes a shower, then dries off.

He puts his BOXERS on, and walks back to the bedroom.

INT. JACK'S BEDROOM - NIGHT

Jack grabs a PILLOW, and COMFORTER from the closet.

He drops the pillow from underneath his arm, spreads the comforter on the floor where the carpet has been cut out.

He then picks up the pillow and props it against the wall. Then walks to the kitchen.

INT. JACK'S KITCHEN - NIGHT

Jack pulls a BOTTLE OF LIQUOR out of the freezer along with a FROSTED LO-BALL GLASS, then proceeds back to his bedroom.

INT. JACK'S BEDROOM - NIGHT

He walks back to his night stand and
pours himself a shot of liquor.

Jack opens the top drawer; and pulls out
an ASHTRAY, neatly stacked with a PACK OF
CIGARETTES, and an ALUMINUM LIGHTER WITH
A VIKING ON THE FRONT.

He sits down on the comforter and lays
back on his pillow. He lights a cigarette
and lays the ashtray and liquor glass
down next to him.

Jack looks at the photographs of him and
Stacy on the wall. He reaches up to turn
off the light.

In total darkness he takes a few drags
off his cigarette and then extinguishes
it in the ashtray.

INT. JACK'S OFFICE - DAY

Jack's desk phone rings, and Tookie is on
the line.

                    JACK
Good day, Lieutenant Jack Hazard
speaking.

                    TOOKIE (V.O.)
Jack, the two towel heads that wanted
Stacy's kidney are here at the club.

They're in the VIP room; with Roxanne,
she's grinding the hell out of them.

                    JACK
Listen to me, stall them until I get
there. Don't let them leave.

Jack hangs up the phone, and rushes out
of the office to his car.

INT. STRIP BAR NAUGHTY NUDE CABARET - DAY

Tookie notices RANJEET and ARMAJEET
exiting the VIP room, with ROXANNE in
hand. Tookie walks over to JEFF the
bartender.

                    TOOKIE
Jeff, give me two VIP passes and two lap
dance certificates.

                    JEFF
Tookie, I'm all out.

Tookie runs to the safe room.

INT. NAUGHTY NUDE CABARET SAFE ROOM - DAY

Tookie reaches into his bra and grabs a
SET OF KEYS. He opens the door, then
closes it behind him.

Tookie then opens up another door which
leads to the safe room. He crouches down,
to unlock the combination of the safe.

Opening the safe; Tookie grabs one EMPTY CASHIER TILL after another, stacking them upside down on top of the safe.

                    TOOKIE
Where in the hell are those VIP passes?

Tookie stands up straightens out his skirt, then exits the safe room.

INT. STRIP BAR NAUGHTY NUDE CABARET- DAY

Tookie approaches ROXANNE, who is chatting up CLIENT #1.

                    TOOKIE
Roxanne, where did those guys with towels wrapped around their heads go?
                    ROXANNE
You mean Ranjeet and Armajeet? They already left, and went to the valet.

Tookie runs past the cashier's stand, then out the main exit.

EXT. VALET STAND STRIP BAR - DAY

Tookie dashes outside, and sees CARL the valet behind the valet stand watching ARMAJEET and RANJEET'S CAR drive off.

                    TOOKIE
Did you see two guys with beards, and towels wrapped around their heads?

                    CARL
You mean the two guys with turbans?

                    TOOKIE
Yeah, with beards.

                    CARL
                 (pointing)
That's them driving off in their car.

Tookie takes a deep breath, sighs, then
sits down on a bench and lights up a
cigarette. Jack pulls up to the valet
stand and exits his car.

Jack tosses his CAR KEYS to Carl. Carl
then gives him a VALET TICKET.

                    JACK
Where are they?

                    TOOKIE
You just missed them. Roxanne is in the
club.

                    JACK
I need to talk to her.

Jack and Tookie go inside the strip club.

INT. STRIP BAR

Jack and Tookie find Roxanne chatting up
CLIENT #1.

                    TOOKIE
Roxanne, I need to talk to you.

                    ROXANNE
Tookie can you wait? I'm with a client.

Jack puts his hand on Roxanne's shoulder.

                     JACK
Roxanne; I'm Lieutenant Hazard, and I
need to talk to you in Tookie's office.
This is important.

                    ROXANNE
Sorry, babe I got to go.

                   PATRON #1
But, Roxanne...

Roxanne kisses him on the cheek and rubs
his bald head, she then gets off his lap,
and blows him a kiss.

                    ROXANNE
Bye.

Roxanne, Tookie, and Jack head to
Tookie's office, while another STRIPPER
approaches CLIENT #1.

INT. TOOKIE'S OFFICE

                     JACK
Now Roxanne, I need to know exactly what
those men told you. Do you know what
happened to Stacy?

                    ROXANNE
Yeah, she got stabbed in her apartment.

                    JACK
Not, exactly. She had her kidneys
removed, and those two guys with turbans
may have done it.

                    ROXANNE
Tookie, why didn't you tell me about
this?

                    TOOKIE
What do I look like? A reporter on the
six o'clock news.

                    JACK
Look, all I need to know is what those
men offered you.

                    ROXANNE
All right, this is what they told me.
There's a girl; who's a diabetic, in need
of a kidney.

Armajeet said they will pay me fifty-
thousand dollars, if I give him my
kidney.

I asked Armajeet what will happen
since my only kidney would be missing.
Ranjeet said: "Don't worry you have two
of them, and the

other one will grow back."

                    JACK
Roxanne, you know people have two
kidneys, just like they have two eyes,
and neither eyes nor kidneys can grow
back.

                  ROXANNE
Hell, if I know. I'm just a stripper, not
a nurse. Ranjeet tipped me three-hundred
dollars, just to rub a cotton swab inside
my mouth.

I thought he was kind of kinky. He then
placed it in a baggie. The same type you
buy weed in.

Armajeet gave me this business card, and
wrote their phone numbers on the back.

Roxanne hands Jack, Doctor Gordon's
business card from her garter belt.

INSERT - DOCTOR GORDON'S BUSINESS CARD:

"Dr. Jeffery Gordon
Transplant Endocrinology
Street Address and Phone Number:
Director's choice
Hand written on the back of the card
reads: Armajeet and Ranjeet
Phone Number(s): Director's choice"

BACK TO SCENE

                    ROXANNE
He said if I was the same blood type as
the girl, I would get paid fifty-thousand
dollars in cash for my kidney.

                    JACK
Roxanne, I need you to help me so we can
catch them in the act.

                    ROXANNE
We? Whose we? I don't want to get
involved, with this shit!

                    TOOKIE
Look, Roxanne you better listen good.
These guys left Stacy for dead.

                    JACK
Roxanne, I am not going to force you to
do anything. However, if you do nothing,
another innocent person is going to die.
Can you live with yourself knowing that?

                    ROXANNE
What do I have to do?

                    JACK
All you have to do is talk to a friend of
mine.

                    ROXANNE
Fine.

                    JACK
Good, tomorrow I'm going to pick
you up at noon.

                    TOOKIE
Now Roxanne, get on that pole and shake
your ass. You still have to pay your
stage rent by the end of the night.

Roxanne gives Jack a hug and kiss on the
cheek, and exits Tookie's Office. Tookie
smiles.

                    TOOKIE
I think she wants to...

                    JACK
Tookie, don't say it. Just give me her
phone number.

EXT. ENTRANCE DOOR OF F.B.I. FIELD
OFFICE - DAY

Jack and Roxanne walk up to the main
entrance. Jack presses down on the
intercom button.

                    JACK
              (in to intercom)
Hey Pat, It's me Jack from Seventh
Precinct. I have someone who needs to
talk to you.

F.B.I. Senior Special Agent PATRICK
BUSCH, responds.

                    PATRICK (V.O. INTERCOM)
No problem, open up the door at the sound
of the buzz.

INT. OFFICE LOBBY

Patrick standing against the wall opens
the door and places his fingers firmly in
Jack's back.

Patrick tall and gangly, stands out with
red hair and gray eyes.

                    PATRICK
Lieutenant Hazard, place your hands
behind your head. You are under arrest.
Jack turns around with a grin.

                    JACK
Pat don't you ever grow tired of playing
games?

                    PATRICK
Relax. How else am I supposed to make you
smile?

Roxanne looks surprised. Jack then
introduces Roxanne to Patrick.

                    JACK
Pat this is Roxanne. She was
propositioned to take part in an illegal
organ transplant.

PATRICK
Let's go to the conference room, we can
talk there.

INT. OFFICE CONFERENCE ROOM

Jack, and Roxanne sit across the table
from Patrick.

JACK
Pat, you already heard what happened to
Stacy.

PATRICK
I'm sorry that she's gone.

JACK
Well, apparently these two guys...
Roxanne what were their names again?

ROXANNE
Armajeet and Ranjeet.

JACK
Yeah, Armajeet and Ranjeet offered
Roxanne, fifty-thousand dollars
cash to sell one of her kidneys.

PATRICK
Is this a joke; are you serious?

ROXANNE
They did at the strip club, I work
at. They gave me this card.

Roxanne hands Patrick, Doctor Gordon's
Business Card.

INSERT - DOCTOR GORDON'S BUSINESS CARD:

"Dr. Jeffery Gordon
Transplant Endocrinology
Street Address and Phone Number:
Director's choice
Hand written on the back of the card
reads: Armajeet's and Ranjeet's
Phone Number: Director's choice"

BACK TO SCENE

                    PATRICK
Whose Armajeet and Ranjeet?

                    ROXANNE
They're doing their medical internship at
University Hospital.

                    PATRICK
Whose hand writing is on the
back of Doctor Gordon's business
card?

                    ROXANNE
That's Armajeet's handwriting.

                    PATRICK
Well if that's the case, we could
prosecute these guys under The National
Organ Transplant Act. A single conviction

carries five years in federal prison.

                    JACK
How should we go about busting them?

                    PATRICK
Through a sting. We are going to need a
search warrant for Doctor Gordon's
office.

                    JACK
What do you need from us?

                    PATRICK
Just the usual. I need everybody,
not to tell a soul. If any of these jerks
get word of what is going on, their
likely to get rid of evidence.

Jack if you could bring Roxanne back in
tomorrow at noon; I need her to fill out
a statement.

                    JACK
We will be back, tomorrow at noon.

Patrick, Jack, and Roxanne leave the
conference room. Patrick walks them back
to the entrance.

INT. OFFICE LOBBY

                    PATRICK
See you tomorrow.

                    ROXANNE
Thank you, take care.

                    JACK
Pat, I appreciate it, and try not to
shoot yourself in the foot.

Patrick locks the door shut and peers out
of the peep hole.

                    PATRICK
Damn, she's hot.

EXT. PARKING LOT OF F.B.I. FIELD
OFFICE - DAY

Jack and Roxanne drive off in Jack's Car.

INT. JACK'S PERSONAL CAR - DAY

                    ROXANNE
You're friends with that goof ball?

                    JACK
Yeah, we went through hostage negotiating
training together.

They drive off.

EXT. VALET STAND STRIP BAR - DAY

Roxanne and Jack pull-up to the valet
stand at the strip club. Roxanne gives
Jack a kiss on the neck then exits the
car and walks through the main entrance.

INT. JACK'S PERSONAL CAR - DAY

Jack pulls out of the strip club
driveway.

Police dispatch announces over his HAND-
HELD POLICE RADIO that there is a hostage
situation at Ready Health Insurance.

                POLICE DISPATCH (V.O.)
Calling all officers in the vicinity of
Third Street and Parker Avenue.
We have a hostage situation, at the
offices of Ready Health Insurance.

                JACK
            (to himself)
Doesn't the pain ever stop!

Jack races to the scene.

EXT. CORDONED OFF STREET READY HEALTH
OFFICE BUILDING - DAY

Jack pulls up to Bill and exits his car.
Numerous POLICE OFFICERS are on scene,
along with NEWS TRUCKS and REPORTERS.

                JACK
Bill what's the deal?

                BILL
Some crazed guy is hopped up on steroids.
He's demanding Ready Health Insurance to
pay for an experimental HIV medication.

Since you're the first hostage negotiator
on site, Chief wants to talk to you. He's
right there in the command post.

                    JACK
I'll be right back. Jack walks over to
the MOBILE COMMAND POST.

INT. MOBILE COMMAND POST - DAY

Jack walks in and salutes Chief
McCormick.

                    JACK
Chief.

                CHIEF MCCORMICK
Jack, just the hostage negotiator we're
looking for. Assistant Chief Andrews has
already devised a plan to end this.

            LIEUTENANT CHIEF ANDREWS
It's simple. You are going to go in
dressed up as a priest.

                    JACK
A priest? Look, I never went to seminary
school.

            LIEUTENANT CHIEF ANDREWS
I know, but the hostage taker wanted a
priest, and as a hostage negotiator you
never say no. You're the priest. You are
going to present these papers to the
hostage taker, Mike Kolowski.

Lieutenant Chief Andrews holds up a set
of TYPED PAPERS.

                    LIEUTENANT CHIEF ANDREWS
You are going to tell muscle bound meat
head Mike Kolowski if he releases the
Doctor unharmed, the City Prosecutor is
not going to press charges.

Plus, the local AIDS Interfaith Alliance
will pay for his experimental HIV
medication.

                    JACK
Is all this even true?

                    CHIEF MCCORMICK
No, but we have to do every thing
possible, so that Doctor Klinger is
released unharmed.

                    JACK
And if he refuses?

                    LIEUTENANT CHIEF ANDREWS
We don't know if he is wearing any
body armor. So, if you have to shoot him,
shoot him in the face.

Lieutenant Chief Andrews holds a BLUE
PRINT of the building, and draws on it
with a MARKER.

                    LIEUTENANT CHIEF ANDREWS
This is the lay out of the building.

Captain Keith Rogers of the SWAT team
will be waiting for you in the fourth
story stairwell. You know Keith, don't
you?

                    JACK
We were on the SWAT team together for a
year, before I was promoted to sergeant.

            LIEUTENANT CHIEF ANDREWS
Good, you will enter the building through
the main doors. On your left will be the
stairwell door. Go up and meet Captain
Rogers and SWAT.

After exiting the fourth story stairwell,
you will be at the elevator landing that
will lead you to the Ready Health
insurance office entrance.

Walk through the double doors and then
past the reception desk. Turn left again
about thirty feet down the main aisle.

There is a glass pane door etched with
Doctor Klinger's name on it.

Knock on the door, and make sure you
announce yourself as Father John
O'Conner. Doctor Klinger and the
kidnapper are in the office.

As a back-up, the surveillance team has
placed a microphone in the air
conditioning duct

of Doctor Klinger's office.

Chief McCormick hands Jack a HANGER WITH
A PRIEST COLLAR, SHIRT, AND PANTS. Jack
walks to the rear of the Command Post to
change clothes.

Jack lastly places his HANDGUN AND
HOLSTER in his waistband at the small of
his back.

Chief McCormick hands Jack a BIBLE and
the papers.

Lieutenant Chief Andrews and Chief
McCormick look at Jack from head to toe.

                CHIEF MCCORMICK
Father John O'Connor it's show time.

                JACK
Let's hope for a divine intervention.

EXT. CORDONED OFF STREET READY HEALTH
OFFICE BUILDING - DAY

Jack exits the command post. As Jack
walks toward the POLICE BARRIERS the
Police Officers stare in disbelief.

                POLICE OFFICER
Is that Lieutenant Hazard?

                BILL
Yeah, that's Jack.

Bill and the Police Officer push aside a
POLICE BARRIER so Jack can enter the
office building.

                    BILL
Good luck Jack.

                    JACK
Thanks, I'm going to need it.

INT. ENTRANCE BUILDING MAIN LOBBY - DAY

Jack enters the building. He immediately
opens the door to access the stair well,
then marches up the staircase.

INT. FOURTH STORY STAIRWELL

Jack arrives at the stairwell landing and
meets KEITH the SWAT Captain. The ten-man
SWAT team are kneeling right against the
wall, with their weapons at the ready.

                    KEITH
Did Assistant Chief Andrews tell you the
plan?

                    JACK
Yeah, how do you want me to go in?

                    KEITH
Before you announce yourself look back
and nod at me. If anything, goes wrong
just yell. Are you ready?

                    JACK
Let's do this.

Keith nods his head to one of the SWAT
team members to open the door for Jack.

INT. FOURTH FLOOR OFFICE ELEVATOR
LANDING - DAY

Jack walks through the fourth-floor
elevator landing. He then gently opens
the lobby doors to the office, with the
SWAT team behind him.

INT. OFFICE ROOM DESKS - DAY

He heads to DOCTOR KLINGER's office and
looks back at Keith as he places his hand
on the door knob.

The SWAT team members are kneeling beside
the office desks and wall. One SWAT
member bumps a desk with three bottles of
soda.

One bottle remains on the desk, he
catches one in midair, the other bottle
he misses crashing to the floor showering
him with soda.

                    MIKE KOLOWSKI (O.S.)
Who's there!

                    JACK
Mike, it's Father John O'Connor from the

Archdiocese. Can I please come in?

                    MIKE KOLOWSKI (O.S.)
You better be no cop, or else I am going
to shoot this quack!

                    JACK
Mike please don't do that. I only want to
talk to you.

                    MIKE KOLOWSKI (O.S.)
Open the door very slowly. If you pull
anything I am going to end it for the
Doctor, and me!

INT. DOCTOR KLINGER'S OFFICE - DAY

Jack enters the office. MIKE KOLOWSKI and
DOCTOR KLINGER; both drenched in sweat
are sitting in the corner behind her
desk.

Mike is holding a gun to the Doctor's
temple. Mascara is running down the
Doctor's face.

                    JACK
Mike, I have good news for you.

                    MIKE KOLOWSKI
Really Father, and what's that!

                    JACK
The District Attorney has agreed not to
charge you, provided you

release the Doctor unharmed.

                    MIKE KOLOWSKI
And what about my AIDS medication? Am I
supposed to fuck off and die!

                         JACK
The local chapter of the AIDS Interfaith
Alliance has agreed to pay for Avataz;
the medication you are in need of.

                    MIKE KOLOWSKI
Is that a guarantee?

                         JACK
Yes, I have the consent decree here
signed by the District Attorney and a
letter from the AIDS Alliance
guaranteeing your medication.

Would you like to take a look at it?

Mike sits up; and orders Doctor Klinger
to stand up and grab the papers, while
holding her by the band of her skirt.

                    MIKE KOLOWSKI
Get up and grab it!

Mike then pulls the band of her skirt
causing it to rip exposing her slip. The
Doctor falls down and sits on Mike.

                    MIKE KOLOWSKI
Now read it!

                    DOCTOR KLINGER
                 (reading the letter)

"Dear Mister Kolowski,

The Greater City AIDS Interfaith Alliance
will cover any and all costs associated;
with the administration and delivery, of
the medication Avataz.

Signed,

Chapter President Miriam De Silva."

                    MIKE KOLOWSKI
Don't stop continue, read the next
letter!

                    DOCTOR KLINGER
                 (reading the letter)

"It is ordered under Title Eighteen, of
United States Criminal Code, that Mike
Kolowski is granted immunity from
criminal prosecution for any and all
felonies that occurred on August 13,
2030.

Provided that any and all hostages
are freed unharmed, and Mr. Kolowski
peacefully surrenders to law enforcement.

Signed,

District Attorney for

the City, Paul Benson."

                    JACK
Mike let her go. It is only right. You
have everything to stay healthy. Allow
the Doctor to leave.

                MIKE KOLOWSKI
Go on Doctor, I got what I needed.

The Doctor stands up and runs out of her
office.

INT. OFFICE ROOM DESKS - DAY

Three SWAT members immediately nab the
Doctor. One places his hand over her
mouth and lay her on the floor.

The second SWAT member cuffs her. The
third with an ASSAULT RIFLE pointed at
Doctor Klinger. They then carry her out
of the reception area.

INT. DOCTOR KLINGER'S OFFICE - DAY

Mike gets up and sits in the Doctor's
chair, placing his gun on the desk.

                MIKE KOLOWSKI
Say Father, can I take a look at that
Bible. I always loved reading Romans
Chapters Five, Three.

Jack reaches out to hand Mike the Bible,

but drops it on the floor.

Jack reaches down to pick up the Bible
only to have his handgun slip out of his
holster sliding right down his back,
landing right on top of the Bible.

                    MIKE KOLOWSKI
You're no priest!

Mike grabs his gun. Jack reaches for his
handgun. Mike fires a shot at Jack
hitting him in his vest, causing Jack to
be thrown against the book shelf.

Mike jumps over the Doctor's desk, and
fires a second shot hitting Jack in his
shoulder.

Keith the SWAT captain rushes through the
door and fires his sub-machine gun,
propelling Mike's body through a window
sill.

LIEUTENANT BRIAN SKINNER; follows Captain
Keith Rogers into Doctor Klinger's
Office, behind Brian are two SWAT
officers who rush Jack out of the office.

I/E. WINDOW SILL DOCTOR KLINGER'S
OFFICE - DAY

One of Mike's legs are on top of the
window sill. The rest of his body is
dangling outside on the ledge. Keith hugs

Mike's shoe with both hands.

                    KEITH
Reach out and grab him!

                    BRIAN
Just calm down and give me your hand.

                    MIKE KOLOWSKI
I don't want to die!

Just as Brian reaches the tips of Mike's
fingers, Mike's foot slips out of his
shoe causing him to fall four stories.

Mike's body hits the pavement. Keith is
cradling the shoe in his arms, with his
mouth wide open.

EXT. - CORDONED OFF STREET READY HEALTH
OFFICE - DAY

Mike's body is embedded in the concrete;
with a pool of blood around him, and the
back of his skull crushed.

                    BILL
Call the coroner we got a body!

Bill and the other Police Officer's faces
are sprayed with blood. Cops rush in and
surround Mike's body.

A SWAT Member slams open the main front
door, followed by four other SWAT Members

holding Jack by his arms and legs.

                    SWAT MEMBER
Get an ambulance we have an officer down!

An ambulance blares its HORN, turns on
its SIREN, and LIGHT BAR, Police begin to
remove the traffic barricades.

As the ambulance pulls up to Jack the
rear barn doors fly open before coming to
a complete stop. The MEDICS roll out the
stretcher.

Jack is placed on a stretcher by the
Medics, and loaded in. The doors are
slammed shut, and the ambulance speeds
off.

INT. - HOSPITAL EMERGENCY ROOM HALL WAY

Jack is being rushed into an operating
room by two ORDERLIES and a NURSE.

INT. HOSPITAL OFFICE - DAY

Misses Dade is sitting at a desk that is
a mess. Medical files and charts, are
piled a foot high. She dials her phone.

INT. CHRISTINE'S HOUSE KITCHEN - DAY

Christine with OVEN MITTS removes a WHOLE
BAKED CHICKEN from the oven. The kitchen
phone rings.

INTERCUT AS NEEDED - CHRISTINE AND MISSES
DADE ON PHONE

CHRISTINE
Hello. Christine speaking.

MISSES DADE
Good evening, is this Misses Carter
speaking?

CHRISTINE
Yes, this is she.

MISSES DADE
I'm Misses Dade, the Transplant
Coordinator, for University Hospital. We
have found a match for your Daughter
Kimberly.

Can you come down immediately for the
kidney transplant?

CHRISTINE
Why yes. Kimberly, my Husband, and I will
be there in less than twenty minutes.

MISSES DADE
When you arrive go directly to the
admission's desk. Doctor Gordon will be
the Lead Surgeon in charge of the kidney
transplant.

CHRISTINE
Misses Dade, we will be there in less
than twenty minutes.

                    MISSES DADE
Please drive safely. Take care.

Misses Dade and Christine hang up their
phones.

INT. CHRISTINE'S HOUSE LIVING ROOM - DAY

David is in his recliner watching
television. Kimberly is playing with her
toys on the floor. Christine runs over
and places her hand over David's
shoulder.

                    CHRISTINE
David, Doctor Gordon found a match for
Kimberly. We have to go to University
Hospital.

                    DAVID
Come on Kim let's go. David, picks up
Kimberly with her doll in her hand.
David, Christine, and Kimberly quickly
head out the door.

EXT. CHRISTINE'S HOUSE - DAY

David, Christine, and Kimberly head
straight to Christine's car.

I/E - CHRISTINE'S CAR - DAY

Christine gets in the front passenger
seat. David buckles up Kimberly in the
back. David repeatedly attempts to start

the engine, but it will not start.

CUTAWAY - JACK HOSPITAL OPERATING ROOM

The SURGICAL NURSE cuts off his clothing and removes his bullet proof vest. A mushroomed bullet drops from the hole in the nylon carrier of Jack's bulletproof vest.

The ANESTHESIOLOGIST inserts an INTRAVENOUS LINE into Jack's arm. Jack's eyes close. A SURGEON stands over Jack.

BACK TO SCENE

                    CHRISTINE
Babe, why won't the car start?

                    DAVID
Hun, I left the light on.

                    CHRISTINE
The light on!

CUTAWAY - JACK HOSPITAL OPERATING ROOM

The surgeon removes a mushroomed bullet from Jack's shoulder which causes him to lose blood pressure, and flat lines. The EKG emits a continuous TONE.

                    SURGEON
Nurse, I need you to pull suction.

The Nurse places the SUCTION TUBE in
Jack's shoulder wound.

BACK TO SCENE

David pulls the release levers for the
hood, and the trunk.

                    DAVID
Don't worry I have a battery charger in
the trunk.

                    KIMBERLY
Mom are we going to have to take the bus?

                    CHRISTINE
No sweetheart, everything is going to be
fine. Daddy needs to jump start the car.

David exits the car.

CUTAWAY - JACK OPERATING ROOM

The EKG continues to emit a continuous
TONE. The surgeon has stopped the
bleeding.

He begins chest compressions. The
Anesthesiologist draws out a liquid from
a VIAL with a NEEDLE AND SYRINGE.

BACK TO SCENE

David connects the ALLIGATOR CLIPS OF THE
BATTERY CHARGER to

the car's battery terminals.

                    DAVID
Christine, I need you to turn the
ignition.

Christine gets out of the front passenger
seat; and runs around to the driver's
side seat, and turns over the ignition
repeatedly.

CUTAWAY - JACK HOSPITAL OPERATING ROOM

The EKG continues to emit a continuous
TONE. The surgeon continues chest
compressions.

The Anesthesiologist places a bag-valve-
mask Ventilator over Jack's mouth and
begins squeezing repeatedly.

BACK TO SCENE

Christine gets the car to start. David
removes the battery charger, and slams
the hood shut.

He tosses the battery charger in the
trunk, slams it shut, jumps in the front
passenger seat, and they drive off.

CUTAWAY - JACK OPERATING ROOM

The EKG shows Jack's heart beating again.

                         SURGEON
That was a close one. Nurse what is his
stat?

                          NURSE
One hundred twenty-six over twenty-three.

                    ANESTHESIOLOGIST
Wake him back up?

                         SURGEON
Yeah, before we lose him again.

EXT. BLOCK FROM THE HOSPITAL/CHRISTINE'S
CAR - DAY

Christine, David, and Kimberly, stop at a
red light. The clouds are dark and gray;
a TRUCK HORN, blares repeatedly.

I/E. CHRISTINE'S CAR - DAY

Everyone stares at the REAR VIEW MIRROR
in horror. A GARBAGE TRUCK skids and rear
ends Christine's Car.

The rear window shatters, projecting
glass throughout out the cabin.

                         DAVID
Kimberly, are you all right?

Kimberly starts wailing with saliva
running down her chin.

                    CHRISTINE
Get Kimberly, we have to run to the
hospital.

David gets out of the car, and pulls
Kimberly out. Kimberly wraps her arms
around David.

David strokes out the broken REAR WIND
SHIELD GLASS out of Kimberly's hair.
Thunder strikes and it begins to rain.

                     DAVID
Kimberly, everything is going to be fine
honey. We are almost there.

EXT. BLOCK FROM THE HOSPITAL/GARBAGE
TRUCK - DAY

The Garbage Truck Driver gets out of his
truck and approaches Christine as she
exits her car.

David; with Kimberly in his arms, begins,
running, towards the hospital.

                  TRUCK DRIVER
Mam, are you all right? I'm sorry my
brakes failed.

                    CHRISTINE
No, my daughter needs a kidney!

The Garbage Truck Driver shakes his head

in puzzlement. Christine runs to catch up with David and Christine.

EXT. CROSSWALK TO HOSPITAL - DAY

David's shoes splashes through the water as he sprints; with Kimberly towards the crosswalk. Christine is close behind.

The SIREN of an ambulance, can be heard from the distance. The RED HAND DON'T WALK SIGN is illuminated, as they run across the street.

An Ambulance screeches to a halt barely missing Christine. They run up the drive way to the main lobby entrance of the hospital.

INT. HOSPITAL LOBBY - DAY

NURSE TANAKA sees David bolt through the door holding Kimberly. Christine is right behind him. The whole family is drenched.

Nurse Tanaka stands up from her chair. David and Christine are panting; David lays Kimberly on the reception counter.

ROBIN SALAS the DESK CLERK lays a file on Nurse Tanaka's Desk and picks up a phone and dials.

                    ROBIN
              (in to the phone)

James, we are going to need a stretcher
in the main lobby.

                    NURSE TANAKA
What happened?

                    DAVID
I'm David Carter, Kimberly's Father.

                    KIMBERLY
Dad can I get up?

                    CHRISTINE
No sweetheart not now.

                    DAVID
We are here for Doctor Gordon who is
going to perform my Daughter's Kidney
Transplant.

                    NURSE TANAKA
Mrs. Salas will call Doctor Gordon's
Surgical Team to alert them.

Two hospital ORDERLIES pull up a
stretcher beside David and Christine.

                    ORDERLY #1
Sorry Mam, we need to lift her.

Christine and David step aside. Robin
with the phone still to her ear instructs
the Orderlies to take Kimberly to the
operation prep room.

                    ROBIN
You need to take her to the pre-operative
room. Doctor Gordon's team is performing
the transplant.

                  ORDERLY #2
Ready? ONE. TWO. THREE. Lift.

The orderlies begin to wheel Kimberly
away.

                   KIMBERLY
               (begins to cry)
Dad what is happening?

David and Christine walk up beside
Kimberly's stretcher, the Orderlies
briefly stop the stretcher.

David bends down to give her a hug and a
kiss. Christine approaches the other side
and does the same.

                    DAVID
Kimberly, I Love you. You are going to
get a new kidney. Everything is going to
be fine.

                  CHRISTINE
Sweetheart you won't have to do dialysis
anymore. We will be right by you when the
surgery is over.

Christine wipes Kimberly's tears away
with her hand, and kisses her forehead.

Kimberly waves goodbye.

Her parents wave back as the Orderlies wheel Kimberly through double doors.

INT. OPERATING ROOM HALLWAY

Jack is asleep in a hospital gown and is wheeled out of the operating room by TWO OTHER ORDERLIES.

Jack and Kimberly, roll pass each other on their stretchers in the hallway.

INT. JACK'S PRIVATE HOSPITAL ROOM - DAY

Nurse Tanaka walks in holding a breakfast tray, and places it on the tray table. She rubs Jack's shoulder, and he is unresponsive.

                    NURSE TANAKA
Mr. Hazard, Mr. Hazard, it's morning. She rubs his shoulder again and he opens his eyes.

                    JACK
Yeah...

                    NURSE TANAKA
Mr. Hazard your breakfast.

                    JACK
Leave it on the table.

Jack, drinks his orange juice, he eats
his eggs and spits it out, then throws
his fork on the tray.

                    JACK
               (to himself)
This is tasteless.

NURSE TANAKA knocks on Jack's hospital
room door, and opens it.

                    NURSE TANAKA
Mr. Hazard there is a person by the name
of Tookie here to see you.

                    JACK
Tookie, send her in.

Tookie walks in with a NEW VISITOR ID and
gives Jack a hug.

                    TOOKIE
Jack, were you hurt bad?

                    JACK
Yeah, I got grazed in the neck and
hit in the shoulder. What happened to the
poor bastard who shot me?

                    TOOKIE
Mike Kolowski the bodybuilder?

                    JACK
Yeah that guy?

                    TOOKIE
He fell four stories out a window and
died.

                    JACK
And the doctor?

                    TOOKIE
She came out without a scratch.

                    JACK
Thank god. Well take a seat.

Tookie pulls up a chair. Jack grabs the
remote, and turns the television on. The
LOGO and THEME MUSIC for "Eye-Witness
Morning Report" plays.

The news anchor John Bellis begins to
read the news report.

                  JOHN (V.O.)
                (on television)
The F.B.I. raided the office of Doctor
Barry Gordon. In what has turned out to
be a real-life horror story of human body
parts for sale.

Our own Elizabeth Danker is on scene with
the story.

They then cut to Elizabeth Danker who is
on scene at Doctor Gordon's office.

ELIZABETH (V.O.)
(on television)
At 6:00 A.M. the F.B.I. stormed the offices of Doctor Barry Gordon.

It appears to be a case of organ transplant recipients being able to purchase human body parts on the black market.

In some instances, medical students stealing organs from anesthetized victims and leaving them for dead.

Armajeet, with a red turban; and Ranjeet with a yellow turban, are seen being escorted in handcuffs out of the office of Doctor Gordon by FBI AGENTS in the background.

TOOKIE
Jack those are the two men who offered money to both Stacy and Roxanne for one of their kidneys!

JACK
Nurse. Nurse!

Jack presses the call button.

NURSE TANAKA
Yes, Mister Hazard.

JACK
Nurse, I need my clothes at once!

NURSE TANAKA
I'm sorry Mister Hazard, but the police
took them in for evidence.

JACK
(to Nurse Tanaka)
How I'm going to get out of here without
any clothes?

TOOKIE
Jack, don't worry; I wear a pair of size
eleven sneakers, and I have a sweat suit
in the car if you need something to wear.

JACK
Tookie, come on let's go. I need to go to
Doctor Gordon's office.

NURSE TANAKA
Now wait a minute Mr. Hazard, you have to
see a Doctor before we release you.

Jack gets out of his hospital bed wearing
his, underwear, hospital gown, and is
barefooted.

JACK
I don't have time for that.

NURSE TANAKA
That is fine please see me at the front
desk. For your discharge papers.

INT. MAIN LOBBY - DAY

Tookie and Jack, follow Nurse Tanaka back to the main lobby reception counter. Nurse Tanaka hands Jack an ELECTRONIC TABLET AND STYLUS.

                    NURSE TANAKA
Mister Hazard if you can scroll all the way down and sign your signature in the box.

I will be back with your personnel belongings.

As Jack signs his discharge papers on the tablet; Nurse Tanaka walks to the rear office to retrieve a PAPER BAG stapled closed, with Jack's name on the label.

Jack lays the stylus and tablet on top of the table. Nurse Tanaka hands Jack the paper bag.

                    NURSE TANAKA
Take care of yourself Mister Hazard.

                    JACK
Thank you, Nurse Tanaka. Come on Tookie let's go.

Jack and Tookie exit the hospital lobby.

EXT. HOSPITAL PARKING LOT - DAY

Tookie and Jack, briskly walk to the parking lot. You can hear the TAP of Tookie's high heels.

Tookie opens his PINK CONVERTIBLE CORVETTE DOORS by REMOTE CONTROL. Jack gets in on the passenger side, Tookie drives out of the parking lot.

INT. TOOKIE'S CAR - DAY

Jack tears open the bag, revealing his WALLET, KEYS, POCKET KNIFE, and CELL PHONE.

                    TOOKIE
Where do we have to go?

                    JACK
I don't know. I have to give Patrick a call.

Jack dials Patrick on his cellphone.

EXT. DOCTOR GORDON'S OFFICE - DAY

Patrick and other AGENTS are dressed in NAVY BLUE WINDBREAKERS with the initials F.B.I. IN BRIGHT YELLOW LETTERS ON THE FRONT AND BACK.

AGENTS are bringing out BOXES OF EVIDENCE AND FILES. TELEVISION NEWS VANS are parked across the street, with NUMEROUS REPORTERS on the sidewalk.

Patrick's cell phone rings.

                    PATRICK
              (into cell phone)
Good day, Patrick Busch speaking.

INT. TOOKIE'S CAR - DAY (MOVING)

                    JACK
              (into cell phone)
Pat it's Jack. Say, what is the address to Doctor Gordon's office? Me and a friend are driving down there right now.

EXT. DOCTOR GORDON'S OFFICE - DAY

                    PATRICK
              (into cell phone)
Sure, its: 659 City Place Avenue Any City, Any State 56231.

INT. TOOKIE'S CAR - DAY (MOVING)

As Jack reads back the address from Patrick, Tookie types it in the car's GPS.
                    JACK
              (into cell phone)
Pat, let me read that back to you. That's: 659 City Place Avenue Any City, Any State 56231, is that correct?

EXT. DOCTOR GORDON'S OFFICE - DAY

                    PATRICK
               (into cell phone)
That's correct.

INT. TOOKIE'S CAR - DAY (MOVING)

                    JACK
Tookie how long is it going to take to
drive there?

                    TOOKIE
About five minutes.

                    JACK
               (into cell phone)
Patrick, I'll be there in five minutes.

EXT. DOCTOR GORDON'S OFFICE - DAY

                    PATRICK
               (into cell phone)
No, problem I'll be waiting for you.

INT. TOOKIE'S CAR - DAY (MOVING)

                    JACK
Tookie where are those sweats and
sneakers you were taking about?

                    TOOKIE
Just pull down the sectional access to
the trunk, it's in my duffel bag.

Jack reaches through the sectional and pulls a PINK DUFFEL BAG, with a pair of WHITE SNEAKERS in the outer pocket.

He unzips the duffel and pulls out a PINK SWEAT SHIRT.

                    JACK
Tookie, I can't wear this pink shit people are going to think I'm some type of fairy!

Tookie slams on the BRAKES of the car to a dead stop.

                    TOOKIE
Fairy? Fairy! This fucking fairy picks up your broke ass from the hospital, when nobody else shows up.

You ask this fairy to give you some clothes and a pair of shoes, and you're bitching about the color when lives are at stake?

                    JACK
Look, I'm sorry I didn't mean it like that. I take it back and I apologize.

                    TOOKIE
You know what's your problem Jack? You're not grateful for half of the shit you already have!

The DRIVER behind Tookie's car, begins to

HONK his horn.

                    DRIVER
              (shouting out window)
Hey, will you hurry it up!

                    JACK
              (to Tookie)
Point well taken. Now can we go?

Tookie, continues to drive. Jack takes
off his seat belt so he can wiggle into
the PINK SWEATPANTS under his hospital
gown.

He tears off the gown exposing his
bandages on his neck and shoulder. He
puts on the PINK SWEATSHIRT,then the
WHITE SHOES and PINK GYM SOCKS.

EXT. PARKING LOT ACROSS FROM DOCTOR
GORDON'S OFFICE - DAY

Tookie pulls up to the parking lot across
from Doctor Gordon's office.

                    JACK
Tookie, this is going to take a while and
I need you to stay here.

                    TOOKIE
That's no problem. I need to polish my
nails anyway.

                    JACK
I'll be back.

EXT. DOCTOR GORDON'S OFFICE - DAY

Jack walks up to the F.B.I. agent, who
stares at Jack from his shoes to the top
of his head.

                    AGENT #1
I'm sorry sir, but who are you? Only law
enforcement officers are allowed in.

                    JACK
                (pulls out badge)
I'm Lieutenant Jack Hazard with the
police department. I'm working with
Special Agent Patrick Busch on this
investigation.

                    AGENT #1
Sure, no problem. Say can I ask you a
question?

                    JACK
Sure.

                    AGENT #1
Are you color blind?

                    JACK
No. Why do you ask?

                    AGENT #1
Oh, it's the pink outfit.

                    JACK
Oh, this? It was red, but I added too
much bleach.

                   AGENT #1
So that explains it. Well, go ahead and
show them your badge. Pat is right
inside.

INT. DOCTOR GORDON'S OFFICE - DAY

Jack enters the lobby and finds numerous
F.B.I. agents walking out with boxes of
files, and agents entering the building
to pick up more.

His eyes perk up when he sees his friend
Patrick talking to his superior; Special
Agent in Charge, Nancy Gurion behind the
reception desk and walks over.

                    JACK
Patrick.

                   PATRICK
Jack.

Patrick smiles.

                   PATRICK
Nancy that's my best friend Lieutenant
Jack Hazard with Precinct Seven. He has
provided us our confidential informant
for this case.

                    NANCY
Hey, Jack come on over.

                    JACK
It's great to meet you. You are the
Special Agent in Charge of the local
field office?

Jack notices the tab of Kimberly Carter's
medical chart sticking out underneath
other files on the counter. He then locks
eyes with Nancy.

                    NANCY
Yes, but not for long I have been
promoted to Executive Assistant Director
for the Science and Technology Branch at
Quantico, Virginia.

                    PATRICK
She is one of the few F.B.I. agents with
a Medical Degree from John Hopkins.

F.B.I. Agent #2 approaches Nancy and
Patrick.
                    AGENT #2
Say Nancy, we found some body organs in a
refrigerator in the back.

                    NANCY
Jack it was good to meet you.

Jack shakes hands with Nancy.

Nancy then walks back to the office of
Doctor Gordon, with F.B.I. Agent #2.

                    PATRICK
I better go back there to see if they
need any assistance. When I'm done let's
go out for a beer.

                    JACK
No problem.

Jack waits a moment, then peers down the
hallway as Patrick enters Doctor Gordon's
office.

He then walks back behind the counter.
Jack looking through the front door sees
two agents talking.

Jack grabs Kimberly Carter's medical
chart, lifts up his sweatshirt and
stuffs, it in his waistband of his
sweatpants.

As Jack adjust his pants, Nancy walks up
right beside him.

                    NANCY
Say, Jack.

Jack snaps his head to the side and looks
at Nancy.

                    NANCY
Sorry, to startle you Jack, but I would

like you to come to my promotion party.
It's this Sunday at Seven-Thirty. Would
you be able to make it?

                    JACK
Just text me the address and I'll be
there.

Nancy kisses Jack on the cheek.

                    NANCY
Thank you.

She then begins caressing Jack on his
sweatshirt close to where Kimberly
Carter's medical chart is hidden.

Jack stares at Nancy directly in the eye,
then swallows his breath.

                    JACK
Thank you, I promise you, I'll be there.

Jack walks away from Nancy toward the
front entrance.

As AGENT #3 walks through the door; with
an empty box, the box rubs up against
Jack's pink sweatpants.

                    AGENT #3
Sorry.

Jack places his hand in front of his
sweatpants.

                    JACK
No problem.

Jack exits Doctor Gordon's office.

EXT. DOCTOR GORDON'S OFFICE - DAY

Jack walks past Agent #1 and AGENT #4,
who are talking.

                    AGENT #1
Say, Lieutenant! Were you able to find
Pat?

Jack turns around.

                    JACK
Yah, I got what I needed.

                    AGENT #4
Take care Lieutenant.

                    JACK
You guys take care.

Jack continues to walk back to the
parking lot. While Agent #1 and Agent #4
continue to talk.

                    AGENT #4
What's with that guy and the pink sweat
pants? Is he a sissy?

                    AGENT #1
He said he used too much bleach while

doing his laundry.

                    AGENT #4
                (nodding his head)
     To hell with the laundry, what that guy
     needs is a pair of glasses.

EXT. PARKING LOT ACROSS FROM DOCTOR
GORDON'S OFFICE - DAY

Jack walks back to the spot where Tookie
dropped him off; he scans the parking
lot. Tookie's Pink Corvette is gone. Jack
calls Tookie.

INT. STRIP CLUB NAUGHTY NUDE CABARET
SAFE ROOM - DAY

Tookie is kneeling by a SAFE removing
MONEY and placing it in a REGISTER TILL;
when he receives Jack's call.

INTERCUT AS NEEDED - JACK AND TOOKIE ON
CELL PHONE

                    JACK
     Tookie where are you?

                    TOOKIE
     Jack, I got called in. I'm the only one
     with a key to the safe room on duty
     today.

     I had to make change for the cashiers, so
     they can start their shift.

                    JACK
How am I going to get home?

                    TOOKIE
Jack, you have my gym shoes you can walk.

Tookie hangs up.

EXT. PARKING LOT ACROSS DOCTOR GORDON'S
OFFICE - DAY

Jack stares at the screen of his phone.
He places his cell phone in his pink
sweat pants and walks over to a coffee
shop in a strip mall.

INT. COFFEE SHOP - DAY

Jack walks in and takes a seat. He pulls
Kimberly's file out from his sweat pants
and places it on the table.

INT. BILL KING'S HOUSE LIVING ROOM - DAY

Bill immediately pulls out his cell phone
and calls Jack.

INT. COFFEE SHOP - DAY

                    JACK
               (into cell phone)
Hey Bill what's up?

INTERCUT AS NEEDED - BILL AND JACK ON
CELL PHONE

                    BILL
Jack, are you all right I just saw
you on the news?

                    JACK
The Feds raided Doctor Gordon's office. I
didn't realize that Kimberly was a
patient of his. I saw her chart sticking
out in a stack of files.

Isn't it Kimberly's birthday today?

                    BILL
Yes, but Christine got the call from the
hospital yesterday for Kimberly's
transplant.

They performed the operation last night
when you were in surgery for your gunshot
wounds.

                    JACK
Really? Who performed the transplant?

                    BILL
Honestly, I don't know who was on the
surgical team. Say, do you have her
medical file with you?

                    JACK
Yeah, I was going to swing by your place.

                    BILL
Well Jack, I got to get back to the
precinct, and you need your rest.

Besides, we are going to celebrate Kim's
birthday when she gets out of the
hospital.

How about if we take a look at her file
tomorrow at your house at nine o'clock?

                    JACK
Sure, thing.

                    BILL
Well listen go home and rest up. I know
Kimberly really wants to see you when she
comes back home. Save that file, and I
will see you tomorrow at nine.

                    JACK
Make sure you tell Kimberly I love her.

                    BILL
Don't worry I will, bye.

Bill hangs up his cell phone.

INT. COFFEE SHOP - DAY

Jack goes into his cell phone's web
browser and places an order through an
on-line transportation network service.

He fills out an on-line request to hail a

driver to drive him to his house. He
places the file back in his waist band.
Jack walks up to the BARISTA.

                    JACK
Good day, can I have a regular cappuccino
to go?

                    BARISTA
Sure, that will be six-twenty.

Jack pulls out his WALLET. He takes out
his CREDIT CARD and swipes it. As he
signs the receipt; a horn blasts, HONK,
HONK, HONK, HONK.

Jack turns around and sees his driver
through the glass door. He grabs his
CAPPUCCINO off the counter and walks out.

EXT. COFFEE SHOP - DAY

An empty SUV parked on the side of the
street blocks Jack's view of the rear
portion of the driver's vehicle.

As Jack's ride slowly pulls forward it is
revealed, it is a HEARSE. Jack walks up
to the Hearse and opens the door.

He enters and sits back in the rear
passenger seat of the Hearse.

INT. HEARSE - DAY

                    DAVE THE DRIVER
Good day, I'm Dave. Are you Jack?

                    JACK
Is this a Hearse?

                    DAVE THE DRIVER
Actually, it is. I'm a full time
mortician and just do this as a side job.
Are you in need of any mortuary work?
Dave hands him a BUSINESS CARD.

                    JACK
          (smiles)
No, not yet.

INT. BILL KING'S HOUSE LIVING ROOM - DAY

Bill stares at his cell phone, he then
reaches for the remote, and turns off the
television. He stands up and walks back
to his master bedroom.

INT. BILL KING'S HOUSE MASTER
BEDROOM - DAY

He gazes at the door of his walk-in
closet. He opens the door and turns on
the light.

He walks past his pressed uniforms all
the way to the back, where his BLACK
DUFFEL BAG lies on the floor.

Bill kneels down on the floor and unzips his bag and pulls out his BALACLAVA with both hands and holds it up in the air.

                    BILL
                (to himself)
I can't go to jail.

Bill pulls out a SUB-MACHINE GUN and pulls back the charging handle. He screws on a SILENCER and loads a MAGAZINE.

Bill lastly places a BRASS CATCH over the gun's ejection port and places it back in the bag and zips it up.

He stands up, walks over to his pressed uniforms, and reaches for his TACTICAL UNIFORM. He takes off his DRESS SHOES and PATROL UNIFORM.

He puts on his tactical uniform, then grabs his COMBAT BOOTS off the top shelf, and zips them up.

I/E. HEARSE - DAY

Dave pulls up to Jack's House.

                    DAVE THE DRIVER
Jack, your credit card has been charged, twenty-two dollars and fifty-one cents.

                    JACK
Thanks, I appreciate it.

Jack exits the HEARSE.

EXT. JACK'S HOUSE - DAY

Jack walks up to his door and removes a
DOOR KNOB HANGAR from a pizza shop off
the knob and punches the combination lock
of his front door.

INT. JACK'S HOUSE - DAY

He drops Kimberly's file on the kitchen
table.

He opens up his refrigerator to find a
half-eaten burrito, a quarter-eaten
hamburger, and an empty two-liter bottle
of soda.

Jack then takes out his cell phone and
the DOOR KNOB HANGAR to order a pizza and
soda on-line from the pizza parlor.

He takes a seat at the kitchen table, and
places his cell phone on the table. Jack
scoots up his chair, reaches down, and
feels one of the legs are uneven.

He looks down at the front leg and sees a
mashed up HUNDRED DOLLAR BILL underneath
the foot of the chair.

As he unfolds it a BAGGIE OF COCAINE lies
over Benjamin Franklin's face. He places
the HUNDRED-DOLLAR BILL in his wallet.

Jack goes over to the kitchen sink turns on the hot water, drops the baggie down the garbage disposal, and pours in some DISH WASHING SOAP.

He shuts off the garbage disposal and turns off the hot water. Jack heads to the bathroom.

INT. JACK'S HOUSE BATHROOM - DAY

He tears off his pink sweat suit, and white shoes, then shoves it into a wastebasket, and showers.

EXT. BILL'S HOUSE - DAY

Bill exits the front door; holding his duffel bag, and walks over to Jim's house.

EXT. JIM'S HOUSE - DAY

JIM QUAYLE is buffing out the front fender of his SUV; alongside two other cars with a showroom luster.

                    BILL
Jim could I borrow your SUV till tomorrow evening? Sarah is with Kimberly at the hospital, and my car is not working.
I have to go on shift tonight.

                    JIM
No problem Bill, I just finished

buffing it out.

Jim walks over and starts up his SUV.
Bill walks around to the driver's side
and lays his bag on the concrete.

Jim gets out of the SUV and hands the
remote control to Bill. Bill gets in. Jim
hands Bill the duffel bag.

Bill places the bag on top of the
passenger seat. Jim reaches out and
clasps Bill's hand, Jim gives him a hug.

                    BILL
Jim you're a lifesaver.

                    JIM
Bill anytime, tell Kimberly I love her.

                    BILL
Jim thanks. I want you, and the whole
family to come over to the house when
Kimberly gets out of the hospital.

                    JIM
Bill don't worry, we will be there. We
can't wait to see her again. Take care.

                    BILL
You too Jim.

Bill shuts the door; rolls up the MIRROR
TINTED WINDOWS, and pulls out of the
drive way. Jim waves good bye.

INT. JACK'S KITCHEN - DAY

Jack now dressed; hears a HOUSE MUSIC RING TONE play from his cell phone on the kitchen table. He sits down at the table and answers.

                    JACK
            (into cell phone)
Hello.

INT. STRIPPER'S LOCKER ROOM

NUDE STRIPPERS are counting their TIPS as they walk in front of Roxanne with their LINGERIE over their shoulders and GARTERS STUFFED WITH DOLLAR BILLS.

Roxanne is smoking a ROACH while she is talking to Jack over her CELL.

                    ROXANNE
            (into cell phone)
Hey Jack.

                    STRIPPER
Can I have that?

                    ROXANNE
            (to the stripper)
Take it.

Roxanne passes the roach to the stripper.

INT. JIM'S SUV - DAY

Bill makes a right turn on red without
turning on his signal. He hears a SIREN
in the distance.

He looks up at the rear view mirror and
notices one of PRECINCT SEVEN'S PATROL
CARS.

INT. STRIPPER'S LOCKER ROOM - DAY

INTERCUT AS NEEDED - JACK AND ROXANNE ON
CELL PHONES

                    ROXANNE
Jack I'm a bit hot and bothered here at
The Naughty Nude Cabaret.

I was wondering if you could come down
for a couple of lap dances, and we could
spend the rest of the night at your
house?

                    JACK
Roxanne, I'll be right there.

                    ROXANNE
See you soon Jack.

Roxanne hangs up her cell phone.

INT. JACK'S KITCHEN TABLE - DAY

Jack places his cell phone down, then turns his head to the sound of someone knocking on the front door.

INT. JACK'S HOUSE FRONT DOOR - DAY

He opens the door for the PIZZA DELIVERY DRIVER.

                    PIZZA DELIVERY DRIVER
Are you Mister Jack Hazard?

He opens the PIZZA BOX and steam begins to roll off the PIZZA.

                    JACK
I ordered the pizza and soda.

Jack opens his wallet and hands the delivery driver a FIFTY DOLLAR BILL. The delivery driver hands over the pizza and TWO LITER SODA JUG to Jack.

Jack drops the pizza box on the floor, then places the two-liter soda jug on top of it.

                    JACK
Keep the change.

                    PIZZA DELIVERY DRIVER
Thank you.

The Pizza Delivery Driver walks back to
his PIZZA DELIVERY CAR parked at the
curb. Jack then steps outside.

EXT. JACK'S HOUSE DRIVE WAY - DAY

Jack shuts the door and the combination
lock BEEPS; he hops into his SPORTS CAR.

INT. JACK'S SPORTS CAR - DAY

Jack looks in his rear-view mirror,
waiting for the Pizza Delivery Driver to
drive off.

EXT. JACK'S HOUSE DRIVE WAY - DAY

Jack then pulls in reverse and peels out
of his drive way.

I/E. JIM'S SUV - DAY (PULLED OVER)

OFFICER JAKE BAKER takes off his MIRRORED
SUNGLASSES and smiles at Bill.

                    JAKE
Christ, if I knew it was you, I wouldn't
have pulled you over. When I ran the
plate in the database, it came up as
belonging to Jim Quayle.

Jake reaches out and shakes Bill's hand.

                    BILL
No biggie, it's my friend's SUV. I was

just going to the shooting range.

                    JAKE
So how is Kimberly doing?

EXT. JACK'S SPORTS CAR - DAY

Jack is cutting in and out of traffic at
a high rate of speed. He zooms past Jim's
SUV whose pulled over on the side of the
road with the window rolled down.

Jake, has his back facing the road,
standing directly in front of the SUV's
drivers side door.

I/E. JIM'S SUV - DAY

                    BILL
Well, Jake I got to make it to the range.

                    JAKE
See you later Bill.

Jake walks back to his patrol car, while
Bill pulls back on to the road.

EXT. VALET STAND STRIP BAR - DAY

Jack pulls up to the valet stand and Carl
hands him a VALET TICKET, he tosses his
CAR KEYS to Carl.

                    JACK
Thanks Carl.

                    CARL
Have fun Jack.

INT. STRIP BAR NAUGHTY NUDE CABARET

Jack walks past TRACY at the cashier
stand.
                    TRACY
Hey, Jack how are you doing?

                    JACK
Is Roxanne on stage?

                    TRACY
She's coming up next.

Jack walks up to the main stage. ALAN,
one of the floor managers pulls up a
chair for him.

                    ALAN
Your usual Jack?

                    JACK
Two please.

EXT. STREET ACROSS FROM JACK'S
HOUSE - DAY

Jim's SUV, slowly creeps up and parks
next to the curb, across from Jack's
house.

INT. JIM'S SUV - DAY

As Bill rolls down the window a SIREN is
heard, prompting him to roll the window
back up.

An AMBULANCE speeds past the SUV, Bill
lets out a sigh of relief.

INT. STRIP BAR NAUGHTY NUDE CABARET

Sitting next to Jack is a WOMAN, middle-
aged, heavy set, wearing a pair of black
overalls, a white long sleeve shirt,
cowboy boots, a crew cut, and no jewelry.

Jack stares at the woman from her boots
to her crew cut.

                    WOMAN
Hey cutie, how are you doing?

                    JACK
Alright, I guess?

Alan arrives with two FLAMING LAYERED
COCKTAILS garnished with: a MARASCHINO
CHERRY, and an ORANGE WEDGE; atop a LACEY
SERVING MACE.

Alan places the first cocktail in front
of Jack. Jack immediately blows it out
and sips it, leaving a liquid mustache on
Jack's upper lip.

Alan takes the second cocktail and places it next to the stage.

INT. JIM'S SUV - TWILIGHT

Bill reaches into his duffel bag and puts on his BLACK LEATHER GLOVES. He zips up his bag and places it over his shoulder and exits the SUV.

EXT. STREET ACROSS FROM JACK'S HOUSE - TWILIGHT

Bill exits the SUV and slams the door shut.

He trips in the middle of the street and drops his bag; he immediately gets up, and slings the duffel bag over his shoulder.

As he walks over Jack's lawn the sprinklers turn on, making him wet. Bill reaches over the patio gate to unlock the latch.

He turns his head to the side as a SIREN can be heard down the street.

EXT. JACK'S HOUSE PATIO - TWILIGHT

He immediately enters and slams the gate shut behind him.

Crouching down he can peer through a hole in one of the wooden slats. A SHERIFF'S CAR speeds by with its light bar on, nearly missing a cat crossing the street.

                BILL
Christ!

        GORGEOUS GEORGE THE PARAKEET (O.S.)
Bill can I get you a beer? Bill can I get you a beer?

Bill slowly turns his head toward GORGEOUS GEORGE THE PARAKEET.

                BILL
Damn, that bird.

Bill unzips his duffel bag, pulls out his mask, and puts it on.

INT. STRIP BAR NAUGHTY NUDE CABARET

                D.J. (V.O.)
Good evening boys. Are you ready to unwrap your brand-new toys?

The STRIP CLUB PATRONS howl and cheer.

                STRIP CLUB PATRONS
Ah-uuuu! Oh Yeah! Woof, Woof.

EXT. JACK'S HOUSE PATIO - NIGHT

Bill calmly walks up to Gorgeous George

who is SINGING in his bird cage.

GORGEOUS GEORGE THE PARAKEET
Feed me Bill.

Bill's eye's shift toward the bowl of
bird feed sitting on the picnic table.
He raises his sub-machine gun, with the
laser sight on.

GORGEOUS GEORGE THE PARAKEET
Feed me Bill. Feed...

Bill shoots Gorgeous George and white
feathers speckled with blood fill the
air, with some landing on Bill.

INT. STRIP BAR NAUGHTY NUDE CABARET

D.J. (V.O.)
It's with great pleasure to present to
you our feature dancer of the night,
Roxanne!

The house lights are dimmed and music is
faded up. Roxanne enters stage left, by
teasing her leg exposing her WHITE
FISHNET STOCKINGS and STILETTOS.

She enters the stage by stretching her
arm upward holding on to the edge of the
open red velvet drape.

Her WHITE, SILK, RHINESTONE STUDDED,
GLOVES, sparkle.

Roxanne pivots on her foot; with her
opposite leg fully extended at an angle
from her side, the toe of her stiletto
slides in an arc on the stage floor.

Now fully visible on stage she comes to a
halt with a smile as the spotlight
shines.

The whole club gives a standing ovation.
Strutting out on in a WHITE MINK COAT,
she turns her back to the crowd. Standing
at attention she drops her coat.

The club is in an uproar. In unison her
legs scissors outwards and places her
hands on her hips.

Turning her head over her shoulder she;
winks, smiles, and then waves as the tips
of her fingers fan out.

Roxanne blows a kiss, then turns back
around. Snapping her stilettos together
she grabs her calves.

With a RED HEART SHAPED STICKER on each
heel Roxanne quickly dips her heels in
and out from the back of her stilettos.

Roxanne gradually hastens the pace of her
heels dipping up and down; to the point
her posterior undulates, whipping the
audience into a frenzy.

Suddenly she jumps out of her stilettos and lands in a full split then slowly lays back on her back.

She back rolls up into a handstand now facing the audience. Roxanne cartwheels stage left landing in a forward split.

She sweeps her rear leg forward, bringing her legs together. Roxanne rocks back and performs a kick up.

She turns to a SAILOR, holding a FIFTY-DOLLAR BILL in his hand. Roxanne charges and slides on her knees, and grabs the fifty-dollar bill out of his hand.

She places it in her PINK GARTER. She takes one of the heart stickers; from her left heel, and places it on his forehead. Then plants a kiss on his cheek.

Roxanne stands up and walks over to a balding OLDER MAN. He places a HUNDRED-DOLLAR BILL in her garter.

Roxanne drops her PINK THONG and places it around his neck. She then calls Alan over to the stage.

                    ROXANNE
Oh, Alan.

Alan then walks over to the stage with a grin on his face. She then places the

ball of her left foot on the shoulder of
Alan's TUXEDO while holding the back of
his head.

Standing on one leg; she gracefully
reaches back to her right heel, and
removes the other sticker, placing it on
Alan's satin lapel.

She dismounts Alan then crawls over to
Jack on all fours and blows out the
cocktail close to the stage.

Rising to her knees she downs the
cocktail and then licks the remainder off
her lips. She then fingers Jack to come
closer.

Jack stands up and places his hands on
the brass rail, and leans forward staring
at Roxanne.

The middle-aged woman sitting next to
Jack taps Alan on his sleeve, then hands
him her CREDIT CARD.

                    WOMAN
Can I have the same thing he's having?

Pointing to Jack.

                    ALAN
One Flaming Jack Hazard coming up.

Roxanne takes the MARASCHINO CHERRY out of the cocktail glass and places it in her mouth.

She then opens her mouth revealing on the tip of her tongue that the STEM, is tied in a knot, and places the stem in Jack's shirt pocket.

She places the cocktail glass back on Jack's table. Shaking her shoulders rapidly the RHINESTONES on her PINK BRASSIER, reflect off of the face of Jack.

Turning around on her knees she places her long flowing hair to the front of her, revealing the CLASP of her BRASSIER.

                    ROXANNE
Take it off Jack.

Jack takes off Roxanne's BRASSIER and holds it up in the air for the whole club to see. Roxanne grabs the brassier back and tosses it on stage.

She grabs the ORANGE WEDGE from the COCKTAIL GLASS and runs to the POLE. Grabbing the pole and making three revolutions she comes to a dead stop.

Leaning back against the pole, she does the standing forward splits slowly raising one leg in the air, while holding

the back of the pole with her hand. She
tilts back her head and squeezes the
JUICE of the ORANGE WEDGE on the tip of
her chin.

Gracefully holding her pose; the juice
begins to drizzle down her chest, her
naval, her thigh, all the way down to her
toes.

A volley of BILLS begin to rain on stage.
Roxanne blushes, smiles, walks to center
stage, and takes a bow. The applause is
deafening.

                    D.J. (V.O.)
Ladies and Gentlemen please give a warm
round of applause, to the greatest dancer
to ever grace the stage of The Naughty
Nude Cabaret. Roxanne!

Alan enters stage right with a FLUTE OF
CHAMPAGNE, hands it to Roxanne. She downs
it. Alan takes Roxanne by the arm and
escorts her down the stairs.

When Alan and Roxanne step back on to the
club floor, Roxanne kisses Alan on the
cheek.

                    ALAN
Your routine has been the best I've seen.

                    ROXANNE
Thanks Alan.

Roxanne hands back the EMPTY CHAMPAGNE
FLUTE to Alan. Tookie walks up to Roxanne
and gives her a hug.

                    TOOKIE
Roxanne you were fabulous.

Jack walks up to Roxanne, with his hands
in his pocket. Roxanne embraces Jack and
gives him a long lingering kiss on the
lips.

                    ROXANNE
Well, are you ready for some fun in the
Champagne Room?

                    JACK
Ready and willing.

Roxanne takes Jack by the hand and they
walk back to the Champagne Room.

EXT. JACK'S HOUSE SLIDING GLASS
DOOR - NIGHT

With the help of a HEAD LAMP, Bill takes
a GLASS CIRCULAR CUTTER, cutting out a
hole in the window of the sliding door.

He takes the GLASS BISCUIT off the
SUCTION CUP, and places it on top of
Jack's picnic table which is littered
with bloody feathers.

He reaches through the hole, unlocks the

sliding glass door, and enters.

INT. CHAMPAGNE ROOM STRIP BAR

Roxanne is straddled over Jack. He slowly slides his hands down to her waist, as Roxanne's hips begin to gyrate on his lap.

Their lips are interlocked when Tookie enters through the SHEER STRIP CURTAIN.

Tookie has a WHITE SILK THONG and a WHITE SILK STRAPLESS BRASSIER draped over one arm, and a pair of WHITE THIGH HIGH HEELS in his other hand.

                    TOOKIE
Roxanne, I brought back a new set of heels.

Roxanne hops off Jack's lap.

                    ROXANNE
Thanks Tookie, just lay it there on the booth.

                    JACK
Tookie, Roxanne is awesome.

                    TOOKIE
Don't get in to any mischief tonight. Roxanne is our star entertainer.

                    JACK
Don't worry Tookie, I'll make bail
arrangements.

                    TOOKIE
Take good care of him Roxanne.

Tookie winks, blows a kiss, and waves bye
to Roxanne. Roxanne waves back, then
turns back to Jack.

                    JACK
Should we get a room?

                    ROXANNE
Honey, we are going to need a lot more
space for the acrobatics I'm going to
perform for you tonight.

How about if we go back to your house.

INT. JACK'S HOUSE BASEMENT DOOR
ENTRANCE - NIGHT

Bill twists and turns the basement
doorknob to no avail. He unzips his
duffel bag; and pulls out his LOCK PICK
SET, then zips the bag up.

Going through the KEY RING OF THE
LOCKPICK SET, on the THIRD SKELETON KEY
he opens the basement door.

He places the lock pick set in his pocket
and closes the door behind him.

INT. STRIP BAR

Jack and Roxanne walk up to the cashier
stand. Tracy hands Roxanne a stack of
bills bound by a WHITE CURRENCY STRAP,
with "ROXANNE" written on it.

EXT. VALET STAND STRIP BAR - NIGHT

                   CARL
Your car is coming right up Jack.

                   JACK
Thanks Carl.

Carl runs to the valet stand to retrieve
Jack's key.

INT. JACK'S HOUSE BASEMENT - NIGHT

The beam of Bill's head lamp illuminates
the dust in the air, as he walks down the
stairs of the basement. He sits down on a
sofa and scans the room with his head
lamp.

The screen of a large television lies
dead center of the basement. The light
shifts up to the sports pendants and neon
sign bar decor.

Bill then pans to pictures of: Jack and
Bill at their promotion ceremony. The
light comes to a rest at Seventh
Precinct's Policeman's Ball with:

Kimberly Carter who is being held by her
Mother Christine and her Father Dave.

Bill is dead center in the photograph
with his arms draped over his wife Sarah,
and Jack.

Two rays of a car's headlights shine
through the basement window. Bill turns
off his head lamp and races to the top of
the staircase.

EXT. JACK'S HOUSE - NIGHT

Jack and Roxanne exit Jack's sports car.
Jack holds Roxanne by the hip, while
Roxanne sinks her hand in Jack's back
pocket.

                    ROXANNE
Gee, Jack your awfully firm back there.

                    JACK
Forget the back, its the front that
counts.

Jack punches in the combination to the
door lock and they enter.

INT. JACK'S HOUSE FRONT DOOR - NIGHT

Roxanne throws her MINK COAT off. Then
pushes Jack against the basement door.

INT. JACK'S HOUSE BASEMENT - NIGHT

Bill has his ear next to the door
kneeling down, and hears a loud THUD.

INT. JACK'S HOUSE ENTRANCE - NIGHT

                    ROXANNE
I'm really thirsty Jack. I don't want my
lips to get dry. Do you have anything to
drink?

                    JACK
Bourbon, Scotch, or Japanese Whiskey?

                    ROXANNE
I'm feeling kind of kinky tonight. How
about some of that Japanese Whiskey? Oh
and by the way; where's the ladies' room?

                    JACK
In my bedroom.

                    ROXANNE
See you soon.

Roxanne kisses Jack. Jack walks over to
the kitchen.

INT. JACK'S HOUSE KITCHEN - NIGHT

Jack goes to the freezer and stacked are
FROSTED BOTTLES OF LIQUOR and two LO-BALL
GLASSES. He takes his thumb and wipes off
the frost off the label of a

JAPANESE WHISKEY BOTTLE. He then walks back to the bedroom with the glasses and bottle in hand.

INT. JACK'S HOUSE BEDROOM - NIGHT

He opens the bedroom door; Roxanne is wearing a WHITE SHEER SILK ROBE, WHITE STRAPLESS BRASSIER, and WHITE THONG.

Roxanne is sitting up, dead center against the headboard of the bed. Jack shuts the door.

He walks over to the nightstand and pours a shot of whiskey in each glass.

Jack kicks off his shoes, tears of his shirt, drops his pants, exposing his bikini underwear, and hands Roxanne a glass of whiskey.

He sits down beside Roxanne; places his arm around her, grabs his whiskey glass off the night stand and raises it for a toast.

                    JACK
Let the good times roll.

Jack and Roxanne toast, and down the whiskey. They both lay their glasses on their nightstands and begin making out. Roxanne straddles Jack and removes her bra.

INT. JACK'S HOUSE BASEMENT - NIGHT

Bill rises to his feet, and slowly opens
the basement door.

INT. JACK'S HOUSE ENTRANCE - NIGHT

A beam of light shines underneath the
door of Jack's bedroom.

Bill steps out into the foyer holding his
sub-machine gun in one hand and gently
closes the basement door with other.

Bill steps over Roxanne's Mink Coat; he
continues towards Jack's bedroom. Mid-
stride Bill's lock pick set falls out of
his pocket.

Bill stands as still as a statue.

INT. JACK'S HOUSE BEDROOM - NIGHT

Jack pushes Roxanne off, with one hand
over her mouth, and with his other hand's
index finger over his lips.

He slowly removes his hand off her mouth,
and reaches underneath his bed, for his
DOUBLE HOLSTER PATROL BELT.

He draws one HANDGUN from the holster and
COCKS the hammer and places it in
Roxanne's hands, while whispering in her
ear.

                    JACK
If anyone comes through that door, shoot
them.

Jack slowly removes the other HANDGUN,
gets out of bed, and walks behind the
bedroom door. He takes aim at the side of
the door and COCKS the hammer.

Bill kicks open the bedroom door, hitting
Jack's gun causing it to discharge into
the ceiling. The top of the barrel breaks
Jack's nose, knocking him out.

Bill drives two rounds in Roxanne's left
shoulder, Roxanne with her right-hand
shoots Bill through his balaclava.

Bill falls forward with his forehead
striking the bed's foot board with a loud
THUD.

                  ROXANNE
Oh my God! Help! Help!

Roxanne jumps out of bed. Her left
shoulder is paralyzed while her left
forearm swings wildly from the elbow
down.

She is still holding the handgun with her
right hand.

As she runs over Bill's body, she drops
the gun on Bill's back and exits the

bedroom. Jack comes to, with his mouth and neck drenched with blood from his broken nose.

Jack trembling crawls to Bill's body. Jack's eyes transfix on the exit wound on the back of Bill's balaclava.

He turns the body over and removes the mask.

                    JACK
Bill?

Bill's two front teeth are knocked out and mouth bloodied. There is a huge bump on Bill's forehead.

A drop of blood drips from Jack's nose into one of Bill's pupils. Jack turns flush and passes out.

INT. JACK'S HOUSE ENTRANCE - NIGHT

Roxanne is screaming all the way to the kitchen.

                    ROXANNE
Somebody Help! Somebody help me!

INT. JACK'S HOUSE KITCHEN - NIGHT

With her right hand she places the phone receiver to her ear then dials NINE-ONE-ONE on the kitchen phone.

INT. 911 OPERATOR'S DESK

The 911 Operator sitting at her computer
terminal receives Roxanne's phone call.

INTERCUT AS NEEDED - 911 OPERATOR AND
ROXANNE ON PHONE

                    911 OPERATOR
NINE-ONE-ONE What is your emergency?

                    ROXANNE
I've been shot!

                    911 OPERATOR
Mam, slow down, help is on the way. You
are on One-Hundred and Sixty Pennsylvania
Avenue?

                    ROXANNE
I don't know! Somebody try to kill me and
my boyfriend, Jack!

                    911 OPERATOR
Who tried to kill your boyfriend?

                    ROXANNE
I don't know who, will you please just
send somebody! I'm bleeding!

                    911 OPERATOR
Mam, please calm down. Officer Dominguez
and the medics are on their way.

INT. JACK'S HOUSE BEDROOM - NIGHT

Jack struggles to push himself off of
Bill's body, and slowly rises to his
feet.

Standing up he wobbles toward the door.
He grabs the door frame to support
himself, but falls forward into the
foyer.

INT. JACK'S HOUSE KITCHEN - NIGHT

Roxanne startled, drops the receiver and
runs to Jack.

INT. JACK'S HOUSE ENTRANCE - NIGHT

                    ROXANNE
Ah! Jack!

She kneels down and cradles his head
close to her chest. Blood is bubbling out
of Jack's nostrils. SIRENS echo
throughout the house.

EXT. JACK'S HOUSE - NIGHT

KNOCK, KNOCK. OFFICER ROBERT DOMINGUEZ is
at the door, with his WEAPON drawn.

                    ROBERT
Police! Open the door! Open the door, or
else I'm going to kick it in!

INT. JACK'S HOUSE ENTRANCE - NIGHT

Roxanne in tears lays Jack back down on
the floor. She runs to open the door
tracking blood all over her white mink
coat.

EXT. JACK'S HOUSE - NIGHT

Roxanne opens the door, and runs into the
arms of Officer Dominguez.

                    ROXANNE
Somebody tried to kill me! My boyfriend
is bleeding!

He grabs her by her right arm and holds
her back. Both of them are illuminated by
the flashing lights of Officer
Dominguez's Patrol Car.

                    ROBERT
Mam! Given this is an active crime scene
I'm going to have to handcuff you till
help arrives!

                    ROXANNE
Are you fucking crazy I've been shot!

                    ROBERT
Mam I don't know you. I don't know what's
in there.

Robert places Roxanne's hands behind her
back and handcuffs her.

145

                    ROXANNE
Ow.

Robert; with his weapon still drawn,
takes Roxanne by her forearm and enters
Jack's House.

INT. JACK'S HOUSE ENTRANCE - NIGHT

They both walk in together. He briefly
let's go of her right forearm to turn on
the hall light.

                    ROBERT
Jack!

Robert holsters his gun, and kneels
beside Jack.

                    ROXANNE
That's Jack Hazard my boyfriend, he's a
cop.

                    ROBERT
No, shit! What the hell happened!

He reaches for his RADIO REMOTE SPEAKER
MICROPHONE clipped to his pocket and
radios Emergency Dispatch.

                    ROBERT
We have a TWO-SEVENTEEN on an officer.

                    EMERGENCY DISPATCH (V.O.)
Officer Dominguez back-up is on its way.

Roxanne is still standing and is
fidgeting.

                    ROXANNE
Officer will you please uncuff me?

SIRENS are blaring, MEDIC #3 and MEDIC #4
enter, with their MEDIC BAGS on top of a
COLLAPSIBLE WHEELED STRETCHER rolled into
the hallway.

                    ROBERT
Get Jack to the Emergency Room quick,
he's an officer with Precinct Seven.

                    MEDIC #3
Right away.

                    ROBERT
Make sure you radio in for another
ambulance.

                    MEDIC #4
Will do.

MEDIC #3 squats down and slides a NECK
BRACE around Jack.

                    ROXANNE
Officer, the man who tried to kill us is
in the bedroom.

                    ROBERT
For God sake lady where is the bedroom?

Medic #3 and Medic #4 lift Jack on the stretcher and wheel him out.

                    ROXANNE
                  (crying)
Are you blind? Its straight ahead.
Will you please uncuff me, I can't feel
my fingers.

Robert walks through the bedroom doorway.

INT. JACK'S HOUSE BEDROOM - NIGHT

Robert stands over Bill's body.

                    ROBERT
Bill!

Robert kneels and feels for a pulse and
is sweating profusely. Multiple SIRENS
can be heard in the background.

                    ROBERT
This is the man who tried to kill you and
Jack!

INT. JACK'S HOUSE ENTRANCE - NIGHT

                    ROXANNE
Yes!

INT. JACK'S HOUSE BEDROOM - NIGHT

Robert marches out to Roxanne takes her
by the arm and sits her on a chair in

Jack's Bedroom.

                    ROBERT
Your telling me that this is the man who
tried to kill you!

Robert pointing at Bill.

                    ROXANNE
Yes!

                    ROBERT
This is the man who tried to kill both
you and Jack!

Still pointing at Bill.

                    ROXANNE
Yes!

                    ROBERT
Do you know who this?

                    ROXANNE
No!

                    ROBERT
I can't believe this is happening!

Robert radios Emergency Dispatch again.

                    ROBERT
Dispatch, I need the Precinct Watch
Supervisor on scene immediately.

                EMERGENCY DISPATCH (V.O.)
Sergeant Stevenson is on the way.

MEDICS #5 and #6, enter Jack's bedroom
with a stretcher.

Roxanne stands from her chair, yells,
then faints, the left half of her white
silk robe is saturated in blood.

                ROXANNE
Are you going to uncuff...

Just as Roxanne drops to the floor
SERGEANT ROGER STEVENSON enters the room.

                STEVENSON
Rob what the hell is going on? Get that
lady on a stretcher.

The medics are about ready to lift
Roxanne on to a stretcher.

                STEVENSON
Is that Bill?

                ROBERT
It sure is.

                STEVENSON
Medic lay that lady on the bed. Put Bill
on that stretcher and take him to the
hospital at once.

                    MEDICS #5
Right away.

The medics place Bill on the stretcher,
and wheel him out of Jack's house.

INT. INTERROGATION ROOM

SUPER IN/OUT - "ONE WEEK LATER"

Jack and Patrick are sitting across from
each other with a desk in between them.
Jack has his nose bandaged up.

                    PATRICK
The crime lab found Kimberly Carter's
medical file on your kitchen table.

I don't know how Kimberly's Medical File
got there, but I am going to assume Bill
left it there on a previous visit.

                    JACK
I say given that he tried to kill me and
Roxanne in my own house, that's a fair
assumption.

Is Roxanne alright?

                    PATRICK
She's going to have to undergo
reconstructive surgery on her shoulder.

                    JACK
And George my parakeet?

                    PATRICK
Ballistics show Bill shot George strait
through the chest. He didn't make it.

                    JACK
What about Armajeet and Ranjeet?

                    PATRICK (V.O.)
Upon arrest they were held in separate
cells. Unfortunately, both of them were
found hanging by their turbans, dead.

INT. JAIL CELL

Armajeet's ties his red turban in a knot
around a metal object. The knot snaps
taut.

Armajeet's feet flutter then slowly come
to a rest. His body sways back and forth.
Ranjeet is hanging in his cell by his
yellow turban.

Blood drips from his mouth, to his beard,
to the tips of his shoes, to a pool of
blood on the floor.

                    JACK (V.O.)
Doctor Gordon did you get him?

EXT. U.S/MEXICAN BORDER VEHICLE
CROSSING - DAY

U.S. BORDER PATROL AGENT WASSERMAN is
standing in front of his Guard Booth and

is holding DOCTOR GORDON'S DRIVER LICENCE in his hand.

Doctor Gordon is sitting in his RED ROLLS-ROYCE PHANTOM, beaded with sweat.

                    PATRICK (V.O.)
I placed, an all points bulletin to the Department of Homeland Security for Doctor Gordon.

          U.S. BORDER PATROL AGENT WASSERMAN
Doctor Gordon could you kindly step out of your car. I just need to do a quick search of your car before you go over the border.

                    DOCTOR GORDON
Sure.

Doctor Gordon Steps out of his car, wearing a THREE-PIECE SUIT.

          U.S. BORDER PATROL AGENT WASSERMAN
By the way Doctor Gordon; can you please turn around, and place your hands behind your back?

                    DOCTOR GORDON
Sir, why do I have to do that?

          U.S. BORDER PATROL AGENT WASSERMAN
You have a warrant out for your arrest by the Federal Bureau Investigation for

violating The National Organ Transplant
Act.

                    PATRICK (V.O.)
He was arrested trying to cross the
border into Mexico.

Doctor Gordon turns around and places his
hands behind his back. His face turns
aghast as the handcuffs are ratcheted.

INT. INTERROGATION ROOM

                    JACK
What about Bill?

                    PATRICK
Bill ... Bill is dead.

EXT. CEMETARY BILL'S GRAVE - DAY

Christine, Kimberly, Dave, and Sarah are
all dressed in funeral attire and are
crying.

Christine is holding Kimberly. The
EPISCOPALIAN PRIEST is giving his closing
prayer.

                    EPISCOPALIAN PRIEST
Blessed be the God and Father of our Lord
Jesus Christ. The Father of mercies and
God of all comfort, who comforts us in
all our affliction.

So that we may be able to comfort those
who are in any affliction, with the
comfort with which we ourselves are
comforted by God. Amen.

The priest hugs: Christine, Kimberly,
Dave, and Sarah, then leaves the family
to grieve.

                    KIMBERLY
Mom, who killed Grandpa? Why did Grandpa
die?

Kimberly looking to Christine.

                    CHRISTINE
Kimmy, I don't know. I don't know. We
will find out once the Police complete
their investigation.

INT. PRECINCT SEVEN LOBBY - DAY

SUPER IN/OUT - "ONE YEAR LATER"

Jack enters the building. Jack walks past
the duty desk where OFFICER BURTON
GARDNER is seated. Officer Gardner picks
up the phone.

                    OFFICER GARDNER
                 (on the phone)
Chief he's here.

INT. PRECINCT LOBBY ELEVATOR LANDING -
DAY

Jack steps into the elevator.

INT. PRECINCT ORDERLY ROOM ELEVATOR
LANDING - DAY

Jack exits the elevator. He continues
through the hall to the precinct orderly
room.

INT. PRECINCT ORDERLY ROOM - DAY

Jack enters the orderly room where he is
surprised by Chief McCormick, Lieutenant
Chief Andrews, and Sergeant Deborah
Casanova.

A single photographer and other officers
are beside them. A camera flashes, and
everyone claps. Chief McCormick walks up
to shake Jack's hand.

                CHIEF MCCORMICK
Congratulations Jack, you were chosen by
the Police Commission to be promoted to
Captain.

            LIEUTENANT CHIEF ANDREWS
Congratulations Captain Hazard.

Lieutenant Chief Andrews walks over to
Jack and takes off his LIEUTENANT BARS,
and pins on his CAPTAIN BARS.

                    JACK
Thanks, I never thought I would make it
this far.

                 CHIEF MCCORMICK
Jack, the courage you have shown the
precinct, let alone the whole force has
been incredible.

              LIEUTENANT CHIEF ANDREWS
Deborah Casanova will be your new desk
sergeant. You know Sergeant Casanova,
don't you?

Sergeant Casanova walks up and stands
besides Lieutenant Chief Andrews.

                    JACK
Yes, I know Sergeant Casanova. We worked
together right after she graduated from
the Academy.

                  DEBORAH
Captain Hazard I look forward to working
with you.

                    JACK
Thanks, I'm going to need all the help I
can get.

                 CHIEF MCCORMICK
Oh, Jack there is somebody else here to
see you.

Tookie walks up to Jack wearing a police

academy sweat suit and a pair of white
running shoes.

                    JACK
Tookie, you're in the Academy?

                    TOOKIE
Yes, they are finally allowing
transgender people in the Academy.

                    JACK
I'll be sure to see you at graduation.

                    TOOKIE
Thanks, Jack.

Jack approaches Chief McCormick

                    JACK
Say Chief, can I talk to you for a
second?

                    CHIEF MCCORMICK
Absolutely.

They walk over to one of the many floor
to ceiling windows that overlook the city
skyline.

                    JACK
So, who is going to be the new Lieutenant
for Precinct Seven?

                    CHIEF MCCORMICK
The commission is looking over a number

of candidates; but ultimately it will be
up to you, to choose.

                    JACK
You mean I get a choice?

                    CHIEF MCCORMICK
Of course, you're the Captain of Precinct
Seven.

                    JACK
For once in my career I finally get a
choice.

                              FADE OUT:

THE END

www.ingramcontent.com/pod-product-compliance
Lightning Source LLC
Chambersburg PA
CBHW030749110726
47900CB00008B/2518